The Last Line

An Anthology by the
Monash Writers Group

Tale

First Published 2019

National Library of Australia Cataloguing-in-Publication entry
Creator: Monash Writers Group, author.
Title: The Last Line: Monash Writers Anthology.
ISBN: 978-0-6483273-9-4 (paperback)
Subjects: short stories.

Cover design by Cathy Larson.

Tale Publishing
Melbourne Victoria

**Other Anthologies by
the Monash Writers Group**

View from the Hill
The First Line

Contents

Foreword

Welcome to the Monash Writers Group's third anthology. After the success of our second anthology, *The First Line*, where we took the first line from stories we liked and used them as openings to stories of our own, it seemed logical to follow up with *The Last Line*. Here we have taken the last line from a book or story and used it as the last line of a new story. We have a diverse membership and the closing lines range from classic literature to pulp fiction. Similarly, the genres our authors have written in range from historical fiction, science fiction, crime, mystery and even mild horror.

Any book like this requires input from many people; thanks goes to our editor, Kim Smith, for elevating our work with her feedback on drafts and proofreading the final manuscript. Thanks too, to our cover designer, on, who, once again, has made our book look hanks also to the Monash City Libraries and

Monash City Council for sponsoring and promoting the Writers Group.

However, the biggest thanks must go to the members of the Monash Writers Group for their hard work and dedication to the project. They spent nearly a year working on this from deciding on the theme, to the launch of the book. Their feedback when workshopping drafts has made this a collective effort. Several authors are being published here for the first time, which is a wonderful start for their writing journey.

We hope you enjoy reading it as much as we have putting it together.

Robert New
Chair, Monash Writers Group

Time Travel

Mube Akinci-Desem

Yesterday, I had to go to the city. I seldom make the trip up to town because everything I need is here in suburbia. Having worked in town for several decades previously, I welcomed the change when I retired a few years ago. Since I do not have any friends living on the other side of the city anymore, I rarely have any need, or want, to make an hour-long train trip to the centre of Melbourne.

However, a couple of weeks ago my son Jason's old bomb, a 1984 Ford Telstar, died a quiet death. It should have been retired a couple of years ago, but my son had an unusual attachment to it, and hence kept it going for as long as he could. His dad bought it from a mate for $250 when Jason got his driver's licence and was itching to have a car he could call his own. Once when it was stolen, he wrote poems and songs about it, until it was found wrecked by the police two days later, leaving him in a rather depressed mood. It needed a couple of thousand dollars to make it roadworthy again. Nevertheless, this time it had died a painless death and had to be sent to the wreckers with a prayer or two.

So, we were left with one car, an SUV, between the three of us at home. Busy people that we all are these days if everyone is in need of the car at the same time we are choked. For example, my husband plays tennis on Monday and Thursday evenings after work, my son plays music on some evenings at various venues around town and if I have a meeting or function to attend on the same evening, we are stuck like Tarzan's Grip on a bench. The same thing can happen during the day when my son and I need the car for various odd jobs or engagements and cannot share the ride.

Hence, we decided to purchase another car to ease into our semi-retirement years. Weaving a thick carpet between several car dealers in suburbia for several weekends it took us a while to choose between a Suzuki Swift, Toyota Yaris, Skoda Fabia and a Holden Barina. There is no need to feel guilty about buying a foreign car anymore since there are no cars made in Australia anyway. Under the pretext of not making sufficient profits, when the Australian government stopped paying them exorbitant subsidies, the Fords and the General Motors, the Nissans and the Toyotas all went elsewhere. The beloved Holden disappeared in no time. Even when they were manufactured in Australia they were still foreign cars, weren't they?

Anyhow, once we made the choice and the price was

right to us, the details of getting the money to the dealer had to be worked out. That's when my husband said, why don't you come into town so we can organise the bank cheque together. He added that it would be a novelty of an outing for me. Henceforth I agreed to meet him in the city at lunchtime the next day.

I got up early, planning to have a leisurely walk to the train station and meet my husband at 12:30 at Collins Place. At 10:30 my son asked me how I was going with my time. I told him to rest easy because I had it all under control while I was also working on my one sudoku for the day. Then at 11:30 I noticed I hadn't configured the walking time and the train journey to actually make it to Collins Place by 12:30. Getting into a panic, I had to ask my son Jason to give me a lift to the station, now please!

I enjoyed the train ride; reminiscing about my workdays. I listened to all the little gossip around me while keeping a firm eye on the stations as we hopped and skipped on our way to the centre of the universe. Just in time, I recalled the loop train and jumped out at Richmond to catch the express one to Parliament.

I was just getting my bearings in order as I stepped outside of Parliament station to be confronted with a massive crowd of people of all ages. It was like a carnival atmosphere, with balloons and placards, with children screaming left, right and centre. I was stuck in between bodies not able to see much else for more than a quarter of an hour till the crowd cleared a little and then I could see a couple of metres ahead of me. There was chanting, applause, speeches and more chanting in front of Parliament House. Although I couldn't see much of what was taking place, the chanting and the placards and the massive crowd reminded me of my student days in the 1970s when we were marching along the city streets and chanting slogans about nuclear disarmament and wanting it now.

For a little while I was a young university student again, feeling invincible, strong and able-bodied, believing in a future full of opportunities. I was healthy, with a photographic memory, with my boyfriend next to me, feeling on top of the world for all who cared.

In this euphoric mood I met my husband exactly at the right corner and we made our way through another route to the bank. We stopped in front of the building that I knew to be the bank. Going through the automatic doors, I was faced with a large open space devoid of any furniture or stalls or barriers. There were lights flashing on and off on the walls all around with people standing in front of them.

It was like a space-age movie. Had I moved in time again? From the 1970s had I moved to 2070 or even further into the future? What was this? A barn out of *Star Wars*? A set of robotic sounds giving directions, or some such defiant orders, confused me even more. Half expecting Darth Vader or Princess Leia to appear out of the corner I looked around in amazement. Holding on to my husband's arm I did not want to lose the one connection with 2019.

Where was I? What had happened to the bank I was certain was right here in this building? The crowds outside were my connection to 1970s, my husband was the connection to the reality I understood, then what was this space here—was it the life as depicted in the science fiction movies in a couple of hundred years or more?

I had to ask the first person I noticed around who looked like someone in charge—maybe they let the individual persons discover for themselves in this future age, maybe Big Brother is watching for any mistakes, maybe this is a test of some sort before they let you settle in one time period or another.

I asked the official-looking young woman in uniform, who looked no more than sixteen, 'Excuse me, I'm looking for the bank. Can you please tell me where the bank is located?'

She smiled genuinely and said, 'You are in the bank. This is the bank.'

'Where are the rows of tellers and the queues of people?'

She grinned this time and impatiently said, 'This is the bank, and there,' pointing at another young woman a few metres away high up on a slope, 'is the teller.' I saw a short podium-like stand with a sizeable young woman towering behind it. She looked like she was out of Grimwald's stories, or a Lilliputian character not quite ready for action.

I had to make the official-looking young woman understand that I was not really from this age, that I was actually from another time. I opened my mouth to say something, but she just beckoned me forward towards the gigantic character ahead. My God! They would not let you speak your mind in this future time. You just have to follow the crowd or do as you are told. If I somehow managed to get to this future time with the aid of some machinery, I should be getting back into my time machine and zoom away. This does not appear to be a friendly time; I should not linger around in a hostile environment. I was in agony! Where was this mighty contraption ready to take me home to my time! Or was this all only in my head? I did not hear any complaints from my husband who was still standing next to me. I held on to his arm with a stronger grip now, anxious not to part from the one little piece of reality we shared together.

Well, we approached the gigantic young woman behind the toy podium. I looked at her and said, 'Is this a bank? And are you a teller?' She laughed and said, 'Yes, what can I do for you?' Then my husband went into action, 'We wish to have a bank cheque made in the name of …' he fumbled in his pocket and came up with the name of the car dealer.

Afterwards, we had lunch at a quaint little Japanese restaurant on Little Bourke Street. I found the quiet humming voices of the other diners around us soothing. Sitting on high stools I felt totally at ease, as if I had been transported to Japan instantaneously. The okonomiyaki and the nabeyaki udon were delicious and healthy. It did not break our budget either.

After the lunch my husband went back to work. We walked side by side a little before he departed. As he hugged me and a gentle peck on the lips, he said, 'See you tonight'. He quickly added, 'Remember, it's your turn to cook today'. Then I walked towards the bookshops along the promenade. I did not take two steps before the chanting and shouting of young voices hit me. I was back in the seventies all over again. For a few minutes I took photos on my mobile phone of the demonstrators and marchers as they walked in groups passing in front of me. Then I gave myself to reading their placards, listening to their chants. As I whispered along with them '*What do we want? Policy on climate change. When do we want it? Now!*' I noticed silent tears running down my face. Here was I grounded on Bourke Street, skipping between the 1970s, 2019, and maybe 2252.

Now, remembering that I wanted to go home, I looked around for any familiar signs; even a simple, solid light pole will do or a nice furry cat. There was none. How do I go home? Wasn't there a train station somewhere close? Will the crowd ever disperse? How will I get home? I just remembered I needed to get home to cook the evening meal. I do love cooking. Should be heading home now? Well, here it goes, I have just bitten my tongue. Swishing warm blood in my mouth I contemplate my fate.

The sun is showing up behind the clouds; its rays are sharp like the tentacles of an octopus awakened by a prey. One golden fang landed on my face briefly, jolting me out of my reverie. Unperturbed, the crowds are still moving along into the distance with their hand-written placards as they chant in regular rhyming patterns. **I wipe the tears and as my mind calms down, my heart resumes its normal rhythm. I feel a surge of positive energy warming me with reassurance and promise of the future that lies ahead.**[1]

---

[1] Last line from *A Resilient Life*, Mariam Issa

Crimson Chamber

Sasha Buntman

My life is in constant flow,
An infinite loop of monthly mayhem
With four transformative phases.
In the beginning, I am the crone:
The dark, new moon of winter.
An eruption …
Gushing out
A volcanic, red river of displeasure.
Even with anticipation,
Expectation
And knowledge of its imminent arrival,
My crimson power
Still startles my spirit.
A release from the torment of the week prior
An uncomfortable welcoming
Of more aching wisdom.
Daggers stabbing deep into the abdomen

Bloated, pulsating and prophetic pressure.
Visionary guidance is here.
Later, I awaken as the maiden:
The waxing moon of spring.
When inspiration and joy begin.
Suddenly, I'm on a new journey
Of self-discovery and development
With pure, action-orientated focus.
With every breath,
Anything is possible.
Soon, I am the mother:
The full moon of summer.
Fertility emanates my body.
A maturity melts within.
Loving emotions surround me.
Bliss radiates all my mundane tasks.
A nurturing essence colours my days.
Finally, I am the witch:
The waning moon of autumn.
Enchantment manifests
An emotional rollercoaster;
A gloomy, moody, magical mess.
I can retreat to my sanctuary
To transcend the agony
Gather insights
Unravel inner truths
And revolutionise who I am.
Next, I am the crone again:
As the phases repeat,

I regenerate.

My beautiful blessing

An existence of pleasure and pain.

A miniature, monthly metaphor

Of our mystical macrocosm and microcosm.

Trust your cycle

and allow Wild Power

to return your sovereignty

and restore the power of the Feminine.[2]

---

[2] Last line from *Wild Power*, Alexandra Pope and Sjanie Hugo Wurlitzer

A Man's Best Friend

Ingrid Fry

Two years had passed since Carmel's heartbreaking decision. It was one of the most agonising calls she'd had to make, to have her beloved beagle, Bandit, put to sleep. She gazed wistfully at the photo of Bandit on the mantle.

Perhaps enough time has passed. Maybe I'm ready to have another dog.

Carmel sat in her favourite spot—a chair at the large wooden refectory table in the kitchen, tapping out words on her laptop. The autumnal sunshine streamed through the French doors, warming her back, and lighting up a vase of red and orange gerberas.

The blaze of fiery colour caught her attention, drawing her eyes away from the grey of the screen. How beautiful, she thought, caressing a delicate petal between a chubby thumb and forefinger.

Carmel's musings were interrupted by a sound of scratching on the mesh of the security door. It was the same sound Bandit made when he had wanted to come inside.

'What the hell?'

Pushing back the wooden chair, she moved towards the front door as quickly as her rotund frame would allow. There, peering at her through the screen door, was a pair of big brown eyes set in a caramel coloured, woolly face. Blue eyes met brown for an instant before the woolly face vanished.

Carmel opened the door and surveyed the courtyard. 'What on earth?'

There was nothing to be seen, other than assorted Australian native plants.

Did I imagine that? It appeared and disappeared in a split second.

Carmel walked along the front driveway looking for the mysterious furry visitor. She checked up and down the street. There was no sign of life other than the ancient grey cat from across the road. It was motley and decrepit. She had nicknamed the cat Greybie, and it stared at her knowingly.

'What's up, Greybie? Did you see a woolly dog?'

Greybie twitched an ear and rolled his eyes. He lurched to his feet, arched his back and hissed at her—all yellow fangs and flinty eyes.

Carmel jumped back in fright and looked behind her for the cause of Greybie's fury. Nothing untoward came to notice. She turned back and Greybie hissed again, with a fixed stare that burned into her brain. A chill ran down

Carmel's spine, and goosebumps erupted over her body. Filled with a sense of foreboding, she turned tail and trundled back inside.

Why would Greybie behave like that? We've been friends for years.

Carmel put the kettle on and made herself a strong cup of tea. The incident had unnerved her, and the sunlit room couldn't dispel the ice in her bones.

I know what'll fix me.

Carmel opened the pantry door and carefully removed a wooden box containing an expensive birthday present from her friend. Direct from Austria, it was an original *Sacher Torte*. The cake was enclosed in a beautifully made plywood box, with dovetailed joints, brass plated metal corners, and an ornate locking clasp. On the lid was a pyrographic inscription which read, *Hotel Sacher, Wein.*

She flicked up the latch and opened the lid; the wood felt warm and slightly rough against her fingers. An aroma of chocolate wafted forth, and her eyes widened as she took in the perfect chocolaty roundness of the cake. It was completely unadorned, aside from a simple chocolate seal—*Hotel Sacher, Wein.*

Selecting her sharpest knife, she ran it under hot water and wiped it dry. Very carefully she inserted the knife into the moist depths of the cake and pressed down. The flawless chocolate coating cracked slightly as she withdrew the knife. She repeated, cutting and removing a generous wedge of the famous cake. The recipe is a state secret, she thought, sliding the slice onto an ornate Wedgewood plate.

The aroma of chocolate and spice was overwhelming. Her mouth watered in anticipation as she studied its composition. Beneath the outer shell of chocolate icing, sandwiched between rich chocolate sponge, were two layers of apricot jam. Using a splade from the set she'd inherited from her mother, Carmel took her first mouthful of this world-famous cake.

Mmmm. Her eyes closed as she savoured the sweet, delicate coarseness of the sponge, the slight bitter tang of the dark chocolate icing, the touch of apricot sweetness, along with exquisite hints of delicious, unidentifiable flavours.

Oh. My. God. It's absolutely the best thing I've ever tasted. I'd seriously kill for something like this!

With the cake consumption successfully erasing her feelings of impending doom, she returned to the kitchen table to continue working on her novel.

~

Scratch. Scratch. Scratch.

'There it is again!'

Quietly she left the table and tiptoed towards the front door. Slowly, she peered around the alcove, and there was the furry face, gazing up at her with big eyes.

'Hello,' she whispered, afraid to move in case he'd take off. In response, there was a wag of the tail and a beckoning tilt of the head.

Scratch. Scratch. Scratch, went a paw against the flywire.

Carmel opened the door hesitantly. 'Now, don't run off on me.'

The little dog stepped inside, sat at her feet and looked up at her with adoring eyes.

'Oh, you little sweetheart!'

Carmel squatted and extended a hand, to which the little dog nuzzled against with obvious delight. Its fur had a curly, dense quality, that felt soft but strangely textured at the same time.

'You've got no collar, no ID, but you're in top notch condition. Where on earth have you come from, little one?'

The dog blinked in response and wagged its tail.

'I'll have to call you something, won't I?'

Carmel paused, assessing the endearing creature before her. 'Archie. That's it. You look like an Archie. What do you think?'

The dog leapt into her lap, Carmel toppled over, and Archie, now standing on her generous chest, enthusiastically licked her face.

'Oh, yuk! Stop with the licking! I guess that means you like me!' She gently pushed Archie off and staggered to her feet.

Carmel opened the front door. 'We'd better find out if you have a home. Let's take you to the vet and see if you've been microchipped.'

At the word vet, Archie ran between her legs, flew out the door, raced up the drive and disappeared. Carmel slowly gave chase, but Archie was nowhere to be seen.

'Damn it!' Carmel walked despondently back down the drive.

I love the little fella. What if he doesn't come back?

A sadness gripped Carmel's heart. Her doggy encounter reminded her of how much she missed having a four-legged friend.

~

Rays of orange morning light filtered through the venetian blinds as Carmel lay in bed thinking about yesterday's events, and her mysterious four-legged visitor. Maybe he'll come back today, she thought, reluctantly heaving herself out of the comforting warmth of the doona.

In the ensuite, she pulled off her nightie and stood in front of the full-length mirror. Large pendulous breasts lay heavily across a midriff that protruded extensively over her lower abdomen which hung apron-like over her upper thighs. Her torso was supported by large, shapeless legs with the texture of cottage cheese.

Carmel stretched out her chubby arms and shook them back and forth. A large fold of skin flapped alarmingly under each of her biceps.

'Bloody hell. Have a look at me. I'm so God damn fat!" With a toss of her black, shoulder-length bob, Carmel turned from her reflection in disgust. 'That's it! As soon as I've eaten the Sacher torte, I'm going on a diet.'

The thought of Sacher torte for morning tea made her hurry to shower and dress.

I'll have a bang-up breakfast. Bacon, eggs, hash browns and toast with lashings of butter. I'll use the high fibre white bread, plus add a grilled tomato —that's pretty healthy. If I'm going on a diet soon, I might as well eat up.

~

Carmel's mouth watered as the aroma of frying bacon and freshly made toast filled the kitchen. She slathered butter on a piece of toast and bit into a crisp, buttery corner.

Mmmm. Delicious!

A trickle of melted butter made its way down her chin, its escape to the floor foiled by her generous bosom.

Damn it! Another bloody stain on my shirt!

Wiping the oil from her chin with the back of her hand, she dabbed at the stain with her other hand, which was equally as greasy.

'Oh, for heaven's sake! Have a look at me!' Carmel stared down in dismay at her grease-slicked shirt. She threw the toast on the bench and attempted to remove her top. Her elbow caught the handle of the frypan which tipped and slid off the hob. Carmel shrieked, and trying to prevent the pan's progress towards her new wooden floorboards, grabbed at it. This had the undesired effect of catapulting the rogue frypan towards her, where she involuntarily entrapped it between her belly and the front of the stove.

'Ow! Owwww!'

Grabbing the handle, she threw the lot into the kitchen sink.

Crash!

The pan sizzled miserably under the drips from the tap, sending a mist of bacon aroma into the air.

Bang! Bang! Bang!

An urgent knocking came from the front door.

I can't answer it. I'm a mess!

Bang! Bang! Bang!

Carmel patted at her hair with greasy hands, tugged her oil-stained shirt straight and headed for the door.

That impatient bastard is going to get a tongue lashing.

Opening the door just wide enough for her head, she peeked out. 'What the hell do you … oh … ah, hello there!' Her eyes widened at the sight before her.

'Sorry to bother you, luv. You haven't seen a brown, curly-haired dog around here, have you?'

Carmel could see six-pack abs through the tight blue singlet. Tanned arms sported impressive biceps and forearms grown from either hours in the gym, or some type of manual trade.

A firey, maybe?

A pair of worn-out denims, heavy work boots, dark eyes, short hair and a chiselled jaw completed the picture. His eyes locked onto hers as he appraised the face peering out from around the door.

Carmel licked her lips and stuttered a reply. 'Wuh, wuh, why, yes … a little dog matching your description has been here on two occasions.'

'He's a terror, loves to run off. Find new friends. Always seems to come back but. If you see him, can you give me a call? I'll give you my number.'

Unable to muster enough saliva to reply, Carmel nodded.

You can give me your number, alright. Phew. I've never seen such a physique. Must live on protein. That's what they do isn't it? Chicken and rice. Not an ounce of fat on him. Solid muscle.

The ring tone *Bad to the Bone* echoed around the courtyard.

'I've got to get this, luv.' He answered his cell with a gruff, 'Yep,' and walked up the driveway talking, his voice deep, resonant and pleasing to Carmel's ear.

He'd better give me his number!

Carmel—hesitant to go outside given her dishevelled appearance—scuttled to the edge of the courtyard and peered around the wall. Her heart sank as she watched him get into a Toyota Hilux and drive off with a squeal of tires.

'Oh pooh, I thought my luck had changed.' She waddled up to the letterbox to check for mail and looked hopefully up and down the street. No sign of the bloke or his dog.

The nearby bushes rustled, catching her attention. A woolly face appeared amongst the banksia flowers.

'Archie!'

Carmel opened her arms and Archie sprang out of the banksias and raced towards her. On reaching her feet, he sat and gazed up at her with affectionate eyes.

'You really love me, don't you, little one?'

Archie snuggled up ever closer.

She patted his woolly head. 'Well, it appears your Dad

is just as gorgeous as you.'

Archie stood on his back legs and pushed insistently against her thighs.

'What is it, sweetheart? What do you want?'

Archie kept prodding, his nails digging into her legs.

'Ow!' Carmel gently pushed him down. He sprang away a few feet, turned and looked back at her with an urgent and insistent stare.

'What?'

Archie trotted back and repeated the procedure, heading off a little further this time.

'You want me to follow you? Is that it?'

Archie gave a sharp yap, jumped up and down on the spot and wagged his tail, his pleading eyes never leaving her face.

'Okay, I get it. Lead on, Archie.'

Carmel followed Archie along the leafy suburban streets, past the local tennis courts, footy oval and up a steep hill. Archie waited for her at the crest, watching the red-faced Carmel huff and puff her way to the top.

'I hope wherever you're taking me is not too much bloody further!' she gasped. 'Feels like I'm having a heart attack.'

Archie was impatient and bounced up and down on the spot, waiting for Carmel to catch her breath. Agitated, he tugged at her tracksuit pants, let go, trotted two houses up and disappeared into a driveway.

Reaching the front gate, Carmel stopped to behold the modern two-story home, surrounded by immaculate gardens. A Toyota Hilux was parked at the end of the driveway, and Archie was waiting at the front door, wagging his tail.

Well, well, well. My luck has changed. Archie's dad is not only handsome, he has good taste too. It appears my wishes have been answered — a dog, and a man!

A sense of optimism swelled in Carmel's heart.

She tottered down the steep drive to be greeted by a frantic Archie, who raced inside barking urgently.

I hope everything's okay. Archie's behaving strangely.

Waiting halfway up the hall, Archie's anxious barking continued, as she rang the doorbell and waited.

Ding dong! Ding dong!

I can't just bowl on in, even though the door is open.

Ding dong! Ding dong!

No answer.

Archie flew back along the polished concrete hallway, skidded to a stop at her feet and tugged at the leg of her tracksuit.

'Okay, okay, something's wrong. I'm coming in!'

Archie raced back up the hallway, skidded around the corner, nearly doing a tank slapper and disappeared. She recognised Archie's bark echoing amidst a cacophony of other yelping.

Crikey, sounds like a kennel out there.

'Hello? Helloooo? Anyone home? I've brought your dog back!'

No answer.

Stepping into the hallway, the first thing that hit her

was the stench. She screwed up her nose recognising the awful stink, and the strange, insistent hissing sound. 'That's gross!'

Her hand involuntarily covered her mouth and nose as she progressed along the hallway, dry retching. 'Oh, God.'

Turning the corner, she reached an open plan living area with a large, modern kitchen. Horrible memories flooded back as she located the source of the smell.

A huge, old fashioned pressure cooker hissed angrily on the stove. Steam gushed forth and the metal bell-shaped weight rattled furiously on top. Someone was cooking beef hearts. The odour hijacked Carmel's senses, returning her to a childhood where she had watched her mother prepare and cook beef hearts for their dogs.

She recalled the sound as her mother slapped the heavy, butcher's paper-wrapped parcel down on the kitchen bench. The rustle of the package, as wrinkled hands unfolded the layers to reveal the gruesome contents. Paralysed and unable to avert her gaze from the grisly sight, she stood and stared in shocked fascination.

Nestled within the blood-streaked folds of paper were three coconut sized pyramids of cherry red flesh, encapsulated by solidified rivers of textured creamy fat.

The flashing of the razor-sharp kitchen knife, as her mother dissected each heart into three sections, the ripping sound as she pulled away the outer membrane. Carmel tried to relax her face from the involuntary grimace that gripped it, as she recalled those images and, the final product—a grey coloured, unappealing meat that made the house reek for days.

The pressure cooker frightened her too. Mother would instruct her to 'keep an eye on it', lest it explode. She had nightmares about the damn thing.

Carmel reached forward tentatively, keeping her head well out of range, and turned down the gas on the hob. The bobbing weight on the cooker calmed rapidly and settled into a gentle rocking motion.

'Phew.' Carmel shook her head in an attempt to dislodge the ghastly memories.

A nearby bank of stainless steel fridges caught her eye as she turned to look for Archie. They were the most impressive fridges she'd ever seen in a domestic kitchen.

Wow! Check out those mothers!

Standing in front of them, they dwarfed even her large girth.

Why on earth would you need such ginormous fridges?

Curiosity won out and she pulled open a freezer door. Stacked inside were hundreds of take-away food containers, all neatly labelled in black texta. Not having her glasses handy, Carmel craned forward and squinted her eyes, checking up and down the shelves. Each container had a date, name and contents.

How organised!

Three large plastic bags sat at the bottom of the fridge. The labels read *Dog Bones.*

So, he does have a tribe of dogs! Maybe there's one for sale.

'Well, hello!' a deep voice behind her said.

Carmel gave a squeal, banged her head on a shelf as she stood, let go the fridge door, and spun around to face the voice.

It was Archie's dad.

Carmel felt her face go hot. 'Oh! Oh, I'm so sorry, I di … didn't mean to … I found Archie, your dog and … and …"

'Thank you. That's awesome!' he said, smiling at her embarrassment.

'I didn't mean to snoop. I rang the bell but no one answered so I thought something was wrong and then I got distracted by the pressure cooker ready to explode and the fridges are the biggest I've ever seen and I couldn't help …'

'Relax, luv! It's okay. Really. What's your name? I need to give you a reward for bringing Scout home.'

'Um, my name's Carmel, and I don't need a reward, it was my pleasure. He's such a gorgeous dog … and his name's Scout then?'

'Yes, and my name's Mitch, short for Michael.' He stretched out a hand and she took it. The warmth and strength of his handshake sent a tingle through her body, and she felt herself flush again.

'How do you spell your name? With a *K* or a *C?*' he asked.

'With a *C.*'

Suddenly aware of her state of dishevelment, Carmel patted at her blouse and tucked a stray lock of hair behind her ear. 'I'm sorry I look such a mess, I left the house in a hurry.'

Mitch flashed her a smile. 'You look pretty damn good to me, luv.'

Carmel's face coloured to maximum intensity.

'Now, before I forget …' Mitch scanned the kitchen bench. 'Typical, no paper. This'll do.' He picked up a lid from a takeaway container, pulled out a texta and scribbled *Carmel* on the lid. 'I'll get you a present and drop it off at your place later.'

'That's a lovely thought, but really, there's no need.'

Carmel rubbed the back of her neck. It ached from hours spent at the computer.

Mitch pulled out a bar stool from the kitchen bench. 'I tell you what—you look really tense. How about I give you a neck and shoulder massage? I used to be a masseur.'

'That would be lovely!'

Oh, Lordie. Thank you, God. This is my lucky day.

'No worries. Hop up on the bar stool.'

Carmel placed her heel on the footrest and hoisted herself up, balancing her large posterior precariously on the narrow stool.

Mitch moved behind her, and she felt the heat radiating from his body. The touch of Mitch's large, strong hands moving over her shoulders, neck and back sent her into a state of relaxed sensual delight. His touch was the only thing in existence, until a sharp pain in her neck jolted her awake. The room spun and she felt herself slip from the stool. Mitch's strong hands supported her as she reached the floor.

Gazing into his eyes, she whispered, 'What happened?'

'You've had a bit of a turn, luv. Don't worry, I'll take care of you.'

Mitch's voice seemed a million miles away. A rapid *tic tic tic* sound approached. It was Archie, his nails clicking on the tiles. He hurried to Carmel's side, leapt onto her chest, and looked down at her with adoration.

Oh, Archie. You do love me so.

Carmel met Archie's intense gaze, and it ignited a lightbulb in her brain.

I know the feeling behind that look!

The splash of drool hitting her cheek confirmed it. The look wasn't love. It was gluttony. Archie coveted her the way she coveted her Sacher torte.

Carmel closed her eyes for the last time, accompanied by the horrifying realisation she was no more to Archie than so much chopped meat.

Mitch stroked Scout's head. 'Good boy! You sure brought home a biggun this time. That's our protein for the next six months. We're gonna have to get a bigger fridge! No more scouting for a while, okay?'

Scout wagged his tail in response and seemed very pleased with himself.

Mitch smiled down at him. **'An excellent year's progress.'**[3]

---

[3] Last line from *Bridget Jones's Diary*, Helen Fielding

Free to Smell the Roses

Sakuntala Gananathan

Being the tallest among the trainees, I was lined up in the last row. I looked down at my shoes I had shined that morning until my freckles seemed to wink back at me. I stood at ease and tried to figure out what the fellow was instructing. Each time he opened his wide mouth I could count his molars, of which one was missing. Perhaps he hadn't brushed his teeth during childhood, or maybe he tripped on his own harsh words. At this thought, I laughed aloud and Mike nudged me. Sweat trickled down me as He Man strode over to us.

'Care to share the joke with me?'

'Sorry, Sir, I couldn't control my cough. Promise it won't happen again.'

He peered at the ID card pinned on my shirt. 'Patrick Thompson, see me after the session is over.'

From then onwards, I could hardly follow his detailed strategies in the event of a sudden invasion, whether by land or air. The others took in every word he uttered. I had thought my remark was not that loud, but when all were silent, with only their heartbeats thumping inside of their khaki shirts, my cackle must have reached the man's ears, specially trained to detect the faintest ruffle while in combat.

~

After He Man discharged us at the end of a gruelling hour, Mike asked me, 'What tickled you to guffaw like a jackass?'

I pursed my lips and hurried over to the trainer's office which was situated right across the quadrangle.

He was a burly man in his late forties and seemed to be engaged in writing out a report, and this gave me time to observe the layout of his room. His table was solid metal and the ashtray was a chunk of grey marble, with cigarette stubs of equal length placed parallel to one another. What a bore … same as his ashtray I thought, but the next instant reined in my thoughts and stood at attention.

His eyes narrowed upon finding me at the door. 'Yes?' The monosyllable was far more expressive than a whole question.

He seemed to have forgotten me and fool I am to turn up here, I thought with regret.

He reached for another cigarette and took his time lighting it. 'Well, Patrick Thompson, how keen are you to learn flying?'

I was overwhelmed with pleasure and unable to believe my luck. 'I'm dead serious, Sir. I'm sorry about this afternoon, and I assure you it was not meant to annoy you, Sir.'

'Well that's forgotten, son.'

Of a sudden the rock-solid ashtray seemed to turn into a jelly-like substance. Boy, you are going to be the envy of the whole batch, I thought. 'Much obliged, Sir. Greatly obliged, Sir,' I repeated, unable to articulate anything more sensible.

My English teacher would advise me, 'Patrick, make your sentences livelier, more colourful,' and I would bring in pots of geraniums and bushes with wildflowers to reinforce my essays, only to evoke amusement in the class. In a trance, I stood there gaping at the man and anxiously waiting to know more about the flying lessons.

He stubbed out the cigarette and focussed his attention on placing it correctly in the ashtray. 'We are short of staff in the Officers Mess. I am sure you could help us out until we find a replacement for the janitor,' he said without batting an eyelid, and then leaned back in his chair to admire the cigarette stubs.

'But, Sir, what about flying lessons, Sir?'

'First, you learn to crawl before trying to fly.' With that he dismissed me with a wave of his hand as though I were a housefly.

Alas! All of my potted geraniums were crushed beyond recognition.

I felt too embarrassed to discuss with the others how I had faired with He-Man, and so rode over to the pub at the next town.

It was well past midnight when I quietly slipped into bed. I could hear someone coughing and another snoring away.

~

'Patrick, wake up would you. He-Man has sent you this suit,' said Mike, showing me a silvery stuff. 'You are to be dressed in five minutes and be ready to take the machine with the Captain.'

My dorm mates gathered around me, one holding my toothbrush and another with my electric shaver. Feeling important, I shooed them away and gulped down the coffee Mike shared with me. Munching on a chewing gum, I struggled into the kit, which seemed to weigh like a ton of steel. I could hardly lift my feet, leave alone walk.

When I ventured to voice my discomfort, He-Man happened to overhear me. He glared at me from the doorway. 'This is a case of flying, you fool, not walking. Make it quick.'

With Mike and the others half-carrying me, I was able to report at the airfield without much delay.

There were three machines ready and waiting for us. Some had already boarded two of the machines, and there were four of us left to take the last plane. I was certain jealousy was oozing out of every pore of the freshmen around me.

While I waited eagerly to take off on my maiden flight, He-Man tapped me on the shoulder. 'Lift your left leg and then your right.'

I did so. Our first lesson while training was to follow instructions without questioning the pros and cons.

'Now, lift your left leg again and then lift your right, before your left foot touches the ground.'

I did so but both feet plopped down on the ground at the same time.

'Repeat!' bellowed the man.

At first, I found it difficult, but soon I did so without much effort. To my amazement, I was rising up step by step as though I were climbing a flight of stairs.

Presently my feet were suspended in mid-air. Whew! I was flying like an eagle, over trees and housetops and over the church spire, the tallest structure in the vicinity.

Down below He-Man, now miniature-sized and powerless, together with my dorm mates were looking up at me in wonder. 'Come down carefully before you hurt yourself!' he called out.

Did I perceive a note of anxiety in his tone? Ignoring him, however, I continued my flight. I could now see fields dotting the ground below. The air was getting cooler as I rose higher and higher.

All of a sudden Mike was beside me, struggling to reach out to me.

'It's amazing, isn't it?' I called out to him. 'I am flying! We are flying!!'

He shook me by my shoulders and shouted, 'What the hell are you trying to do? Come down, fool!'

I was in a daze and stepped down slowly with my arms stretched out, left foot first and then the right.

'What's come over you, Patrick?' Mike said angrily. 'See how you have dirtied my bed, jumping up and down.'

I rubbed my eyes, and it took me a while to realise that I had my bedsheet coiled around my shoulders.

'By the way,' Mike added, 'He-Man asked me to inform you to forget about going to the Officers Mess. What's up, Patrick?'

'Thank God, he has cancelled the dinner invitation. I am now free to smell the roses in my soup bowl.'

'Dinner invitation, my foot!' jeered Mike, as he followed all the others out of the dormitory.

I reached for my electric shaver and frowned at my reflection in the mirror. **'Don't ever tell anybody anything. If you do, you start missing everybody.**[4]

---

[4] Last line from *The Catcher in the Rye*, J.D. Salinger

A Secret No More

Ruth Kweitel

Ninety-seven-year-old Betty became a little nervous and distracted during the current affairs activity she was attending, in the aged care facility in which she lived. She looked out the window and saw a perfectly blue sky and stillness among the branches of the garden bushes. She also spotted an empty seat in the garden. Betty then turned to her ninety-five-year-old friend, Dorothy, whom she was sitting next to, and whispered, 'The bench seat under the willow tree looks very inviting. Let's have our afternoon tea outside.'

'What a good idea. I can't wait for this activity to finish,' Dorothy whispered in reply. Both women had forged a close friendship two years ago, not long after Dorothy had moved into this supported community. As soon as the activity finished, both ladies began to make their way to the garden.

Dorothy was the first to speak. 'This'll be a pleasant

change from afternoon tea in the lounge room. Occasionally there are days when there's a smell of urine wafting around, and I can't bear that. We can also avoid the crowd hovering around the tea trolley. Don't get me wrong Betty, I'm not complaining. I know the staff do their best and this place is nicer than some places I've seen and heard about, which is why I chose to come here.' Betty quickly spotted one of the nurses. 'Jenny, would you mind bringing our afternoon tea outside?'

'Not a problem Betty. It's nice and warm in the sun and the fresh air will be good for both of you,' Jenny replied with a warm smile.

'Thank you dear. You're very kind.'

No sooner had they sat down, their afternoon tea arrived. Betty began to devour her slice of fruitcake while Dorothy continued with the discussion that had taken place in the current affairs activity they had just left.

'Betty, what do you really think about that politician's new relationship, not to mention what he has done to his wife and daughters and impregnating that young lady? I think his behaviour is appalling, don't you?' Betty sat silent for a moment and became lost in her own thoughts. After a couple of minutes of silence, Dorothy put her hand on Betty's knee and shook her. 'Betty, are you alright?'

'Yes, just give me a minute. I need to have a mouthful of my tea and then I'll get back to our conversation.' As she started to sip her tea, her eyes began to fill with tears.

'Whatever's the matter Betty? Have I upset you?

Don't you feel well?'

'I'm sorry Dorothy. I'm alright. The problem is the discussion we're having. It took me back to another place I hadn't thought about for such a long time.'

'We don't have to continue this conversation if it's upsetting you.'

'Dorothy, I'm going to let you in on a secret I've been carrying for the last seventy-nine years. I never even told my late husband Jim, nor our two children. The politician's affair brought back some very sad memories for me; memories I thought I'd pushed into the back of my mind and thought I would never think about, ever again.'

'Betty, you don't have to tell me.'

'Yes, I know, but now I really want to. I think it's about time.'

'In 1939 I had a boyfriend, George. We were both very young, I was seventeen and he was eighteen. George joined the army as soon as the war started. On his last night before his deployment, we spent a few hours together in a hotel. George proposed and I accepted. He asked me to wait for him to come back and we would then get married. He wanted me to keep our engagement a secret until his return, when he could buy me a ring.' Betty took a tissue from her sleeve and dabbed at her reddening eyes.

'Oh dear. Betty are you sure you're alright?'

'Yes Dorothy. I've kept this secret for so long, I think now's the time to tell it, so maybe I can eventually have some sort of peace of mind. Anyway, George and I had our secret engagement and I was so happy.

A few weeks later, I discovered I was pregnant. In George's last letter to me, he told me he was being redeployed again, this time to Alexandria. I decided not to tell him about the baby as he was nervous about going and at the time, I thought he had enough to worry about. When I told my parents I was pregnant, they were furious. All they could think of was the shame and embarrassment I brought upon them. Just as I was about to start showing, they packed me off to New South Wales, to a home for single, pregnant girls. They made sure I was far enough away from Melbourne to keep my pregnancy hidden. I went to a place run by nuns who were mean and horrible. I stayed there until the baby was born. George and I had a son. I named him David.' Betty began to shiver and weep softly into her tissue.

Dorothy put her arm around her and held her while she cried. 'I'm so sorry Betty. What started out as a current affairs conversation has revived such sad memories for you. If only I'd known, I would never have continued the conversation.'

'Dorothy, I need to get it out. It's been my secret for so long, I don't want to keep it hidden anymore. My husband Jim has passed away, so I can't hurt him. My parents forced me to give David up for adoption. I never saw him after the birth. The nuns whisked him away before I could get attached. My parents felt the shame for the rest of their lives, especially my mother. I was heartbroken and guilt-ridden. When I returned to Melbourne I got on with my life, waiting for George to return, however that was not to be. He was killed in action in Alexandria. I was heartbroken again. Our engagement remained my secret. Three years later I met Jim and after a short courtship, we married. My parents demanded that I never speak of the baby, ever. They were terrified that if Jim found out, he would leave me. I abided by their wishes and Jim never found out about him.'

'Oh, good lord, I feel very sad for you and I'm so sorry,' Dorothy responded while dabbing her eyes with a tissue.

'Dorothy, there's more to the story and I do want to tell you, but I'd like to finish my cup of tea first. My mouth has become very dry. That happens when I get nervous.'

'Betty you needn't feel ashamed or embarrassed anymore. It was wartime then; our lives and the times were very different. You certainly weren't the only one to have a baby out of wedlock. The home you were sent to had other girls in the same predicament. Thank goodness times are different now. Just look at the situation with some politicians. They get judged because they have affairs and babies while still married, not because they have a baby out of wedlock with a new partner.'

'That's true. I don't think many women realise how lucky they are. Women can choose whether or not to marry and, they can have their babies out of wedlock and nobody bats an eyelid. Unfortunately, I can still remember the look of horror on my mother's face when I told her I was pregnant. That look I'll take to my grave. My mother was such a hard woman. I promised myself I would never treat my children like she treated me. That place she sent me to was so depressing, so much so that a few girls ran away while I was there. They never came back. God knows what happened to them. I remember a couple of girls took their own lives after their babies were taken away. It was awful. I thought I'd pushed these memories so far away I never thought I would ever think about that time in my life, ever again.'

Betty then focused on finishing the remainder of her cup of tea in silence. As soon as she had finished, she dabbed at the beads of sweat emerging on her forehead. 'I don't know about you but, I'm starting to feel warm,' she told Dorothy.

'I think you're just feeling a bit nervous. Betty, would you like me to call nurse Jenny?'

'Don't make a fuss. I'll be OK.'

'Betty, I hope you don't mind my asking but, did you ever try to find David?'

'Yes, I did. The search was very difficult because I had to do it secretly. I didn't start looking until after Jim had passed away, which was thirty years ago. I tried to contact the home where I was sent, but it had closed. When I discovered that, I thought finding David was not meant to be, so I let it go for quite a long time. After many years had passed, I began to have difficulty sleeping. If I woke in the middle of the night, I started thinking about David and wondered what had become of him. That thought became more frequent and it got to the stage I couldn't stop thinking about him. I started to become very nervous as I felt I was becoming consumed by it.

'My children sensed something was wrong. I knew what was wrong, I just I couldn't tell them. They pushed me to see a doctor, so I went to my GP and asked for some sleeping tablets. I couldn't sleep and was beginning to feel and look exhausted. It was probably the best thing I ever did. My doctor probed a little bit into my personal life and my secret about my illegitimate son was revealed. I explained that I started to search for David and hit a dead end when I discovered the home had closed. He gave me some contacts to follow up, which might help my search. I made many phone calls, always from a street phone box so my children couldn't accidentally hear any of my conversations. Thank God there were still plenty of phone boxes at the time. I eventually discovered that David was adopted by a childless couple who lived in New South Wales. I begged for their last known address, then got myself a post office box and sent David a letter. I received nothing for a long time and had almost given up on the search. One day, when I was least expecting it, a letter finally arrived. David invited me to Sydney to meet him; he said he couldn't travel. I told my children I needed a holiday. They readily accepted that and off I went to meet David. I asked him to meet me in the foyer of the hotel, where I was staying and told him what I would be wearing so he could identify me.

'David was a few minutes late. I got quite a shock when I saw him enter the foyer. He walked in using sticks and wore callipers on his legs. There was no doubt he was my son—he was the image of his father. I'd almost forgotten what George looked like. I couldn't believe I'd found my son, after all these years. I felt an immediate urge to hug him as I rushed up to greet him, however he was quite reserved, so I felt I had to keep my distance. That did hurt. I needed to remind myself *I* was looking for *him* and that he hadn't been looking for me. We sat down in a quiet corner of the lobby so we could get to know one another. David asked me about the circumstances of his birth and adoption. I held nothing back and told him everything, including how much I loved his father who was killed in action during the war. He seemed very surprised when I described the shame I'd brought to my family and how they never forgave me.

'I asked David to tell me about himself. He told me he was four-weeks-old when he was adopted and that his parents named him Peter. He didn't know he was originally named David. He remained an only child and his parents adored and doted on him. In primary school, he contracted polio and because he couldn't play sport, he read books to occupy himself. He must have been a good student because he won a scholarship to university and became a history teacher, then worked his way up to becoming a school principal. When I asked him whether he had a wife and children, he said he chose to remain a bachelor because he didn't want to be a burden on anyone. He claimed to be very happy and that he knew about his adoption from a very early age. I told David that he had a half brother and sister. He remained silent, which I found rather hurtful. He didn't seem particularly interested.

'After that, David got ready to leave and told me that all his life his parents had lived with the fear that his biological mother might come looking for him and that my contacting him had caused them considerable distress. He asked me not to contact him again; he didn't want any more contact. He said he was pleased to have met me but felt an obligation to his parents and didn't want to cause them any more pain. He told me that he understood my situation, but I don't really know if he meant it. I've abided by his wishes. My rights went out the door when I gave him up. I'm happy I saw him and know that he's happy and loved by his adoptive parents. I now feel exhausted Dorothy. I hope you don't mind if I go inside and have a lie down for a while. I'm somewhat relieved my secret is out.'

Dorothy hugged her friend and took a deep breath as she watched Betty slowly wander back into the building.

That same evening, Betty failed to attend the dining room for dinner. They always sat at the same table together. Dorothy found that very unusual and began to worry. She asked one of the nurses to check up on Betty. When the nurse entered Betty's room, she found Betty motionless, lying on her bed with her eyes closed and a slight smile across her lips. She had passed away in her sleep. Dorothy was distraught about the unexpected death of her close friend and spent the next few months grief-stricken. She frequently reflected on their conversation. It was all she could think about after Betty's death. After several months Dorothy had a small epiphany. She suddenly realised the strength of character Betty had as she was able to move on with her life, despite two tragic losses. Dorothy came to admire this strength and, as a consequence, decided if Betty could cope, so could she. From that day on, Dorothy began to move on with her life; she stopped deliberating over the past and began to live each day as it came, with a renewed strength she didn't realise she had. **It was a way into the future and a way out of the past.**[5]

---

[5] Last line from *Blood Ties*, Jennifer Lash

We Can Still Be Friends

Marlene Laurent

I stood outside the school in my miniskirt and T-shirt and felt sweat begin to pour off my brow. I could have blamed it on the Melbourne summer heat, but I knew the real reason was likely nerves and my racing, irrational thoughts. Maybe I didn't really want to be a teacher. What if after three years spent studying to get a teaching qualification I'd be no good in this job? *Just walk through the gate with confidence like you used to when you were a kid.*

'Are you okay?' I heard someone say as they strolled past me.

'Yes,' I said with bravado. 'I'm a new teacher. This is my appointed school.'

'Oh, just follow me to the staffroom. You'll be right.'

My legs trembled, but I made my way to the staffroom. I heard the Principal talk to me as if through a fog, as she told me I'd be teaching a Grade 2 class. I assured myself that Grade 2 would be okay.

I arrived in my classroom before the pupils. I saw a stage at the front of the room and a blackboard and rows of desks. The teacher's desk was in front of a cupboard that had once been a fireplace. The desk was small, old and battered with only one small drawer. The walls were bare, and to me the room seemed cold and clinical, unlike classrooms I'd been in on teaching rounds. I looked in the cupboard under the blackboard and found a box of white chalk and a box of coloured chalk, my tools for teaching. The blackboard was clean. Each day I would have to fill it with work for the students to complete. I took a stick of chalk from a box and trying not to shake, so I could do my best writing, I put up something easy for the day. I finished with some vivid colours of chalk and decorated my first lesson with a few twirls.

Then I went out and asked the Infants Mistress if there were any aids or equipment for me to use in my lessons. She showed me a box with Cuisenaire rods for teaching maths and the fordigraph machine. This was used for running off worksheets I designed and made myself.

I went back into the classroom and stood there ready to greet the students. I heard their noise and chatter getting closer. When they started streaming into the room I wondered how I would get them to quieten down.

I noticed a small bell on the teacher's desk. After a couple of loud rings, I got their attention. The silence was even more confronting than the noise.

I introduced myself and then told them, 'You may sit

with your friends this week, and if you can work quietly and get your work completed, you won't be moved.' My mind raced, trying to think back to sessions when I'd been a student teacher. I was to be firm but always approachable.

I noticed one boy who didn't seem to know anybody. He sat alone at the last empty desk.

'What's your name? Do you have any friends at this school?'

'Harry. It's my first day. It is the third school I've been to,' he said without further elaboration.

'So, you and I are both new.' I smiled at him reassuringly and wondered if he shared my nerves. This was to be the first of many conversations I would have with Harry.

The class had thirty-five students, twenty-five of whom were boys. The first day whizzed by and was enjoyable despite my nerves. It was fun to hand out new pencils, textas, and books. The students wrote their names and the date at the top of the page and completed work from the board. Most students took time to make their first page attractive. At the end of the day, I had them put their work in the green tray on my table, and that night I corrected it and tried to match a name to a face. The one name I did know already was Harry's, and I was surprised to see that his page had his name and date on it, but not much else.

I soon learnt that Harry wasn't an ideal student. He spent each class constantly interrupting and distracting the others. 'Hey, Jason want to play footy at lunch?' Then leaning over and giving Mary's plait a tug. 'Ouch, Harry, that really hurt.' He completed nothing. I began to wonder why his behaviour was so disruptive and why he was completely disengaged from learning.

It wasn't long before I realised that he couldn't read or write, and, of course, he didn't want the other students to know. He hid behind being the class clown and made the other students admire him by being brave enough to misbehave.

One day when the pupils were doing *Show and Tell*, the classroom door flew open and in marched Harry wearing a snorkel in his mouth and flippers on his feet. The whole class burst into laughter. I kept a straight face, although it was difficult not to smile. 'Good morning, Harry. You're late again. Remove the snorkel and flippers and put them on my desk.'

'But I want to show them.'

'Too late,' I replied.

After some coaxing he complied and went to his seat where he continued to distract the others. This was typical of Harry, who had a great sense of humour and knew exactly how to get the students' attention and interrupt my lessons. As the days went by, I began to think either he or I would have to leave. It was such a challenge to teach in that environment. One day I asked him to stay after school for a chat.

'Harry, I know you can't read or write. I want to teach you both. But you must tell me if that's what you want to do and if you're ready to learn. I need you to stop wasting my time in class and allow me to teach the other students.'

He gave me a quizzical look and wandered off down the schoolyard and out of the gate, shrugging his shoulders. A few days passed, in which he continued with his usual attention-seeking behaviour. But then one morning as I was getting ready for work, I heard the front doorbell ring. It was Harry.

'Good morning,' he said, as if it was the most natural thing in the world that he would turn up at my house. He smiled. 'I just wanted to say hello.'

'I'll see you at school,' I muttered, taken aback by the fact that he knew where I lived. 'Meet me at school and we can chat then.' I closed the door and my husband asked, 'Who's at the door?'

'One of my students,' I replied.

'Oh, that's strange. What did he want?'

'I guess I'll find out today.' We kissed each other goodbye and went to work.

Instead of being late that day, Harry was in class on time and sitting at his desk. As I went down the aisle he said to me, 'I'm ready to learn.' This was a real breakthrough but also a challenge. How was this going to happen?

He hung around at the end of the day.

'Aren't you going home?' I asked.

'My mum is at work and she won't be home until late. I want to come home with you so you can teach me to read.' I realised then that his mother and father were separated, and she had to work to make ends meet. Most of the pupils at the school were from a different socio-economic background and were well off financially—their mothers didn't need to work.

I phoned his mum to ask her permission. This was the beginning of an amazing friendship.

'I have to do some shopping on the way home. You can come if you like?'

And so Harry came to the supermarket with me. As we walked up and down the aisles filling the trolley, I had the feeling of someone following us, so I stopped and noticed a tall man looking very serious and obviously not shopping. 'Are you following me because I have Harry with me?'

'Yes.'

He was a store detective. I introduced myself and asked if Harry had been stealing from the store.

'Yes, he has.'

Without even thinking about it I blurted out, 'I'm Harry's teacher and I'll make sure he doesn't shoplift again.'

As we moved down the next aisle, I asked Harry how he paid for the items he took.

'I don't. Me and a mate just put things in our pockets and sneak out.'

'You can be arrested for that; it's not a good thing to do. From now on I want you to agree you won't do it again. You can choose three things to buy whenever we go shopping. Okay?'

'Okay.'

Shopping became a ritual, and whenever Harry wanted to talk, he'd ask, 'Can we go shopping?'

That first afternoon when I sat down with Harry to help him learn to read and write, I wondered how I could make our lessons interesting and meaningful. I remembered a competition I'd seen at Kentucky Fried Chicken. 'Hey, Harry,' I called out from the kitchen, 'would you like to win a can of coke?'

'Yes'

'Well, KFC has a competition. Would you like to enter? You have to write the reasons why you like KFC in twenty-five words. If you win you get a free can of coke.'

Harry wasn't sure at first, but I assured him we could do it together. When he won, he was so excited he knocked on the door especially to show me his can of coke.

One Saturday when I was reading *The Age* newspaper, I noticed an article about a group of teenagers who'd been caught and convicted of various petty crimes. I showed my husband. 'I think one of these boys is Harry's brother.'

One of them *was* Harry's brother, and he was now in a government program which focused on a new approach to help teens not reoffend. The offenders were living in a shared house instead of juvenile detention. The house just happened to be in a street I drove along to get to my house. Every day on the way home from school, Harry would beg me to let him talk to his brother, whom he hadn't seen for a while. This is why some days we stopped and Harry would jump out of the car, and go in to see his brother. One day, Harry's brother came outside and introduced himself to me. 'Hi, Miss. Thanks for teaching Harry to read and write.' He put his arm around Harry. 'Go with your teacher. She'll make sure you don't end up in a place like this.'

Now that Harry was motivated to learn, he quickly became the best pupil in my class, and no longer interrupted my lessons. He came to my home every day after school in order to continue his lessons. Together, Harry and I thought up fun topics for him to write about, and we often went to the library and borrowed books he was interested in. Others in the class noticed the change in Harry, and so did some teachers. I was criticised by them for taking an interest in Harry and his learning, especially for including him in my private life. I heard them talking in the staffroom, saying it was a bad move to get personally involved with students. 'Is she going to take the whole class home?' one teacher wondered.

'She won't last very long in teaching,' another suggested.

No one stepped up to help the struggling student or the new teacher, not even the Infants Mistress.

Despite all this, I survived my first year of teaching and maybe I did make a difference. When Harry was allocated to his Grade 3 class, I went and discussed the best way forward for him with his new teacher. She was open to my ideas and agreed with my suggestion that she focus on his learning and make him toe the line in class, and I would be there in the background to continue to support him.

Towards the end of my second year at the school, a senior teacher who would become the new Principal at another school approached me in the staffroom. 'Congratulations on your promotion,' I said.

'Thanks. I have a proposition for you to consider. Come with me to my new school. I know you've moved house, and I'd like to have you on my staff. My new school is closer to your new home.'

When I told Harry I would be leaving, he was upset. 'But what will I do without you? Please don't go!' he begged.

'You're fine now,' I assured him. 'You keep working hard in school and we can keep in touch.'

After I left he would still call and say, 'Can we go shopping?' I'd pick him up and help him with his homework and his reading. Borrowing books from the local library was still his favourite activity. In return, Harry would help me in the garden.

Harry finished primary school and went on to high school, but he became disengaged again and was known as a nuisance. I visited and spoke to them about his background, but they weren't interested and said they'd be happy to see the back of him. I soon learnt that he'd started to wag school.

I researched and found a school that provided a less

structured approach. I asked if they could take him, but they had a two-year waiting list, so Harry had to stay at his current high school. We remained in contact.

One day the phone rang. 'Hi, can we go shopping?'

'Sure. I'll pick you up after school.'

As we wandered around the supermarket he confessed why he really wanted to see me. 'I stole a car.'

'Why did you do that?'

'Got off the train late at night and decided we could hot-wire it to get ourselves home from the station.'

'You could have rung me. I'd have come and picked you up.'

'But I didn't drive it,' he said with a 'not guilty' look on his face.

'You were there, and you were in the car, so you're guilty. What happens next?'

'I'm going to court in a few weeks.'

'You know if you get a conviction there are many jobs you may not be able to apply for.'

'Really, like what?'

'Teaching, being a policeman, although I guess you wouldn't want to be one of those!'

We both laughed.

'I can't guarantee I'll be able to help you. You did the wrong thing, so you should take the punishment. But I'll write a letter to the judge on your behalf.'

And so I did. In the letter I explained Harry's circumstances and the relationship we had. His parents were separated, and his father had a drinking problem.

His mother had been left with the responsibility of bringing up three boys on her own, although she had since re-married and so Harry had a stepfather. He told me he was not very fond of his stepfather. Neither of them contacted me about him, although on weekends I would encourage him to spend time at home with his family. Harry told me that his father had not been interested in keeping in contact with him either.

I said I would guarantee Harry didn't reoffend.

The judge gave Harry a warning. Harry completed his two-year probationary time without being charged with any summary offences. He continued to come to our home, and he became a member of the family. I had my first child, and Harry was like a big brother for her.

Harry left school the day he turned fifteen. I was upset about this, but then again, I knew I had always tried my best to help him.

Harry disappeared from my life. Many suggested he'd been ungrateful, and they wondered why I'd bothered to help him. I didn't think of it like that. I'd always wanted him to live his own life and stand on his own two feet.

One day, years later, the phone rang and a voice said, 'Hi.'

I recognised the voice straightaway. Harry and I chatted as if we'd just talked a week ago. He asked how I was, and he told me he had some news to share with me. 'I've just had a little girl, and I wanted you to know. Her name's Emma.'

We had the most amazing conversation. After that,

we kept in contact, but there were lapses where we didn't chat. I learnt that Harry had gone back to school as a mature age student and had become a qualified horticulturist. He worked as a landscape gardener. Maybe our gardening sessions had given him a love of plants.

Once again, we lost contact until Harry found me on Facebook and invited me to be his friend.

Today, I love seeing what Harry is doing via his Facebook posts. He hasn't lost his sense of humour, and I chuckle at the videos he posts on YouTube.

In Harry, I had made a friend for life.

So, I believe in the words: People belonging to different groups have many things in common.

They can still be friends.[6]

---

[6] Last line from *From A Barred Window*, Katarina Fares

Maysin-DickSee Line

Sung-Ju Suya Lee

'Turn back. Exiting Zone Twelve. Return to cluster core in Zone Zero.' The dual-cabbed ute's hologram dashboard reports. The analogue voice more a scream than a directive. The ute spears through a roaring desert gale. The door logo, P.R.O.T.E.K.T., becomes a blur. Its meaning lost in the tempest.

In a nanosecond, the windshield displays the same message. She can see clearly through the blinking, but irritating message. Flashes faster than the rotating wipers. Each squeak of the wipers grates her psyche. The sand scrapes across her vision. Rubbing in her irises. Her growls barely escape through her grinding teeth each time the words flicker on. Some strands of her long black hair get caught and cut off between each clash of her molars.

Wires dangle from the engine in the ceiling. The ripped hole lets the guts of the engine slip and block her vision. The hot wiring still burns her fingers. Blisters bubble over each scorch.

'Do not leave the safety zone. Do not enter Sa-Vigge Territory.'

The wind shear brands the ute, and concusses the driver. The swirling gravel strikes the front window. Each pebble nicks the glass quicker, without breathing space now. Her puffing hits critical panting. Her tongue slips past her lips and slops against her chin like a dog. The growls turn to muttering moans. *I know I have my brain still.*

'Final warning. Do not enter Zone Thirteen.'

What she can't see through are her tears. She doesn't know why there are wet streaks down her face. Her fingers tremble and touch them. It scalds not only her fingers, her heart flutters as the heat scorches on each pulse. The sweat from her palms adds to the water on her face.

There are no other vehicles in sight. No one dares.

'Stop. Entering Zone Thirteen.'

Why is my face wet? It's not raining, and the ute has a solid sealed roof.

'The cluster capsule will not be able to protect you. Turn back.'

She doesn't heed the warning as she switches to manual. Her hands strangle the joystick between her knees as she jostles to max. The dirt under her fingernails matches the dirt before her eyes. Only her fingers carry the reek from the inferno.

The dirt path leads straight into a black mass of nothingness. Ramming the grey cells into space. The sky devoid of stars. The dirt isn't even on the ground. It's not the tyres kicking it up, it's the wind. It scoops it up and blinds you. The P.R.O.T.E.K.T. controls the weather, even outside of the civilisation dome. The dirt pelts the ute at the same angle that a butcher slices gristle off a steak. To her ears, searing the sizzling flesh. The dual tri-orbital wipers shovel it off and make two perfect circles. She doesn't see the drying blood on the inside of the screen. She only looks out from the driver's seat. The ute chokes from despair.

'I'm … *cough* … not going to make … it.'

Who said that? These words reach her ears, but her brain jams to a halt. The hologram dashboard audio pointer hovers at the zero-marker. It can't be the wind talking. Nor, the dirt. She can't lose control of her brain, not yet. No, those are old myths from the Eternity Records, many eras ago. The high school history lessons suffocate the more it tries to stay alive in between her neurons in her brain. *How can anybody lose their brains?*

The sirens still blare behind her on the deserted dirt road. Echoes louder in her ears. The red and blue lights parade inside the ute. Growing like the sirens. The joystick stops against the ute's steel front panel. Her arms extend almost beyond her body. The electric body seatbelt restricts her from leaning forward. This shield harness has a strict mandate to always preserve the occupants. It glues her to the seat.

The hologram dashboard flickers on and off the further away from Zone Twelve. Unsure, she tries to adjust the front panel, but her hand goes through it. Grasps at the angry void below the hologram dashboard. Defiant in its nothingness.

A gloved hand snatches her hand. Blood-stained, its only evidence of life.

She lets out a shriek, and wakes up the sleeping, daring souls out in Zone Thirteen. Her squawk bounces back at her, and she swerves the joystick away from the strange hand. The tyres gouge out the dirt off the road. Swerves right, then left. The gravel turns to rocks. Smashes into the windshield. The front glass holds, but with gashes deeper than a devil's excavation. The bowels of the planet, saddled with the scars from endless caesareans, no longer whispers from its depleted ore mines or the hollow caves of fool's gold. One of the rotating wipers breaks off. No time to wave good-bye.

That gloved hand loosens its grip.

She wipes the blood off her sweaty hand, life from this stranger, but the stain remains on her khaki uniform. The blood bleeds onto the grease and sulphur on the uniform. The oily stench shouts across her tainted soul out to the cosmos. She stares at this person lying beside her, as she takes back her own hand. Long black hair peeks out from under the stranger's helmet.

Who is this person? Remember.

Try to remember.

~

The President Washington Solar Bank's alarm impales her eardrums as it wails across the city.

Without a breath of time, the metropolitan alarm system activates, and challenges the sanction of the P.R.O.T.E.K.T. Each cluster rings its troops, gathers the hordes back behind its gates. The herd obeys, flocks of shuffling feet seek the signs of safety in the floating hologram monitors, the drones and the blimps. Droves of scared eyes don't dare to blink. They do not want to miss the scanning. The moon centres itself at its perpendicular eye. Murky as the shadows creep in and chase the faint away. No stars to guide it back down. Shit!

Never the one to let her compatriots go down and cop any hefty slammer time or worse, she hits her hologram dashboard. The hologram steering wheel vanishes and spits out a joystick. It bristles in her hands. The cold joystick rages under her palms. A thunder times three roars over the city alarms. Count … one … two …

Three khaki-uniformed motorcycle riders, with full helmets and knapsacks, race towards her car.

She revs up the joystick. It hisses against the sirens. Opens the door hatches, front and back of the ute.

~

'Warning! Zone Thirteen.' The windshield glows red. 'Sa-Vigge breach.'

A circular loop warning signal pulses out of the front screen. A faint flash is the only indicator out of the exit of the civilisation dome. She barely registers its significance.

The 'Sa-Vigge' breach?

She scans the barren desert looking for clues or signs for the … what? Yes, the 'safe harbour'. The night offers no help. Black pillows obscure the moon. The stars were swallowed and sealed at the Primitive Tick-Tock of Time. The myth of the Maysin-DickSee Line crashes earthbound.

'Violation of the President's Act. Citizen cancelled. Dweller records deleted—' The hologram dashboard reports. Its pitch overwhelms her brain. There is no room to think.

'—Good riddance.' She hears her own words. The secret silence echoes off the ute's steel interior. Deadening time inside her brain. 'I don't want to … dwell … reside … uhmm … uh?'

Her tongue twists, slides over her lips, eager to make the next sound. Each wet tongue follicle tangos. Waits for a partner. A pairing between vibration and knowledge. Nothing comes. Silence from her brain.

She checks the rear-vision display on the flickering hologram dashboard. All clear. The red and blue lights dimmed into extinction back at Zone Twelve. The red curdles to orange. The glow from the civilisation dome reflects inside the ute. A heavy hue of forgotten sunsets settles against the windshield. The siren's silence never penetrates her brain. The grey matter withers away in losing cell connection with the gathering dirt the tyres gouge out.

She looks at the stranger, unsure if the person is breathing. She innately checks the gloved hand for a pulse. Blood stains from before rests in her blind spot. More crimson contamination spreads over her pant legs. She catches a glimpse of her own image on the hologram dashboard mirror. The dark circles under her eyes smear across her face. The sleep-deprived are covered in dirt and filth. The Furnace drains life from the workers. She doesn't recognise herself.

What's my … name? Remember.

Damn it, remember.

~

'Kitty, they were waiting for us!' The woman takes off her helmet and half-slides inside the ute. Her red hair blurs her eyes. 'We couldn't get all the solar energy sticks for the clinic— Agghhh …'

The woman screams. Louder than the oncoming two motorcycles' roars. Then, the sound abruptly cuts off. The words get lost in the blood. The red liquid gurgles up and sprays the inside of the ute. Blood squirts out of bulging eyes. Those eyes peer out through her red hair. Her tongue half-bitten off, still clutches in the horizon between the top and bottom row of teeth, soiling hope inside.

A massive mechanical claw bites into her back. Each talon sinks deeper. Tears into her flesh under the khaki uniform. Her lungs collapse. It crushes a heart into a million fragments of lost promise. The chain tethered at the end of the claw yanks the person back to the torpedo-gun at the top of the solar bank. The whizzing chain clanks against the side of the building, bounces the lifeless body. More bones broken as a message for the herds below.

Kitty inhales the mist of blood. She chokes. The gag reflex doesn't come fast enough. Her scream comes out first before the redhead's blood. She reaches out. The air slaps her hand away. The whoosh-blowback of the claw throws distance between the nanoseconds.

Another claw shoots out with teeth ready to bite and mangles

~

Kitty steadies her hand on the joystick. The vibrations make the ute feel furious. The motor going at max. Her blisters call out to the nightmare without release. She keeps wiping the sweat off her palms. The uniform eats the perspiration and the blood stain floods the pant legs.

The orange sours to yellow inside the ute. Turns the blood stain to brown. Turns her khaki uniform into mud vomit. The electronic harness flickers on and off. Her body sore from slamming into the side of the ute. Every bone feels the enraged bumps the tyres send up.

The effort of blinking away her tears does not work

the same as the wipers on the front windshield. She squints at an unfamiliar object up ahead. Unsure, she slows down. It's a bullet-ridden road sign just like in the old movies. Before they were banned. Wiped from the memory banks of the world. It reads, 'Maysin-DickSee Line'.

The yellow ferments into green inside the vehicle. Attacks the blood stains black. The green light floods her irises, but never hits the back of her brain.

'All data has—been—deleted. Your—life memories—'

She has no idea what this road sign means, as she looks beyond the empty horizon. The hologram dashboard threatens to shut down. Flickers more off than on. She looks down at where her hand is … Remember …

The green coagulates into blue. It smudges on the lip of gangrene. Clears itself of festering colour lines. Clear blue emerges. Kitty thinks that she has seen this colour before. When she had looked up, before the civilisation dome was created, there was this colour up above our heads. It made everyone … happy. *What was that?*

The motorcycle helmet falls off the person's head lying beside her. Long black hair drapes around her face. Then, cascades off. This stranger's face looks like her face. But, how can that be?

Remember …

~

Kitty, get these to Mama and the others at the clinic. Cough.' She unstraps her knapsack. Puts the other knapsack on top. The blood from the salt and pepper woman dribbles down to the bottom knapsack. It seeps into the seams of the zippers. A river of red runs down along the zig-zag into the seat. Her shaky hands wipe it, but smears it across towards Kitty. 'They can't make us work in the Furnace any longer.'

'Stop talking, sis. I got to get you help.'

'The Furnace is killing us. Kitty, are you listening? Make sure no one follows you. You remember the map of the underground maze, right?'

'Shhh … Don't talk, sis. We'll be home soon.' Kitty holds a blood-soaked cloth on her sister's neck. One talon's irate scratch lives across the side of the neck and cheek.

'Cough. Get the others to the safe harbour.'

'Please stop talking. There's no such place.'

'I heard … cough … cross the Maysin-DickSee Line. Cough. It's there. Cough.' Blood leaks out of swollen lips.

'Oh god, oh god. Stay with me. Stop talking trash. These are just legends.'

'If Mama doesn't get these, if they get caught …'

'No, they are all safe there. Mama will treat everyone who has fall-out cancer.'

'Listen, Kitty. The radioactive waves are getting stronger the closer we dig to the core.'

'Sis, stop talking. I'll get us home.'

~

The 'Maysin-DickSee Line' sign sees dust as the ute zooms past.

The blue plunders into indigo. It blends the inside of

the ute into the surrounding night. The indigo darkens the entrails of the ute. The eyes snag on nothing in the horizon.

Kitty stares at her sister's frozen face. Her sister blinks. A red light ignites inside the irises. The chip wastes no seconds. A flicker of an image, '100'. Kitty stares into her sister's eyes. *What does that mean?* Dust gathers inside Kitty's grey matter. Before her sister can blink, again, it flashes to '99'. Then, '98'. '97'. Pulsating down. The ebony eyes fade toward ivory. Kitty thinks of a song from her campfire childhood days. Numbers counting down. It's counting down to '0'. Nothing? That's less than 'one'. Right?

Tick-tock, tick-tock, the gears hustle inside her brain as she tries to remember. The cogs lose oil as the 'Maysin-DickSee Line' road sign fades.

… Death.

She slams on the brake. Both feet sweep past her body's limits, the tips of her boots push into the front steel panel. The deep scuff marks rival the windshield's gashes from the flying rocks. Her exhale forces the gale back, for a nanosecond. With one hand, she turns the joystick 180 degrees back to the clinic, back to the civilisation dome, back to P.R.O.T.E.K.T. Back to their Mama. Her sweaty palm glides over the top of the ball on the joystick. Her knuckle shreds against the front steel panel. The joystick licks up the leaking crimson. With the other hand, she wipes the last of her tears.

The hologram dashboard goes dark. It whines its last

wrath as it dies. No final cough from the computer. The electronic harness's light expires last. The indigo transpires into violet. It floods inside the ute. A rose opens its petals.

The engine, dead. Kitty eyes the back of the rectangle board on stilts. This board hides the civilisation dome from view. The lights still twinkle through the bullet holes. The kaleidoscope effect casts a rainbow shower through the pock-marked holes. Her head doesn't move as it is cemented in place by her brain. Her irises click over. The chip sputters and swipes right. The countdown fires up. The signals inside her brain only murmur. Her irises, excited by the bright changing colours, open and close continuously. Never blinks. A blip of a thought travels across Kitty's brain. *These stars are so beautiful.*

Her hands fall off the joystick. Flop beside her legs. Her fingers no longer feel any burn. Her finger brushes against her sister's face. She never sees her sister's eyes close, as the irises flicker red numbers down to nothing.

Kitty's irises twinkle '100'. Then, '99'. '98'. The cold air oozes into the ute. The tyres idle in the dirt. The wind piles up the sand on the ute, against the starless night. In the near distance, the other small mounds rest silently. Kitty's eyes mirror her sisters. The irises lost in bleach. There are no savages past this line. Breaches that become eternal graveyards. Kitty and her sister. And, the rest.

Beautiful, beautiful savages.[7]

---

[7] Last line from *Savages*, Don Winslow

The Farm

Austen Lehmann

The child opens its eyes to the darkness. Today is the child's birthday. Excitedly he sits up and waits for his eyes to adjust. With sleep still hanging heavy over him, he flicks the covers aside and shuffles to the light-switch. The golden glow of the light temporarily blinds him. As his eyes recover, he looks expectantly about the spare room: a small single bed with nightstand; a low, squat set of drawers; walls covered not with posters or hand-drawn pictures, but with a cracked and faded eggshell coloured paint. There is nothing else.

His shoulders slump with disappointment and he trudges back to the bed. As he reaches underneath for his slippers, he feels something solid. He bends down and sees a dark shape. He pulls the shape out: a square box wrapped in blue paper, a ribbon and card attached. He removes the card and reads, *For you, my son. Dad.* A gift from his father, he can hardly believe it. He smiles and rushes with gift in hand to open the door. 'Mum, Mum!' he yells. There is no answer. Closing the door, he returns to the bed and sets the box on the unmade bed. Within moments the ribbon and blue paper are strewn across the floor. Before him sits a brown cardboard box with a wavy black line making its way across the exterior. A closer look reveals the black line to be a procession of ants. With wide eyes, he opens the box and pulls out its contents, placing them one by one on the floor: four panes of glass, a metal frame and plastic lid, a box of sand, and a dark plastic container. He brings the container close to his face and sees that the darkness is moving, that it is, in fact, a swirling mass of ants. Finally, he pulls a piece of paper from the box: *Create your very own Ant Farm in seven easy to follow steps!*

The house is still quiet, so he sets to work, putting the ant farm together.

Following the instructions, the child sits on the floor and begins. Firstly, he assembles the frame; he then slides the glass panes into place; next, the sand goes into the glass enclosure, followed by the addition of some water, which he pours from the glass he has on the nightstand; he then attempts to empty the container of ants onto the sand, but the ants do not budge. Even a shake of the container does not move them. He has to put his hand in and scoop them out. Many stick to his hand and their movements and tiny bites frighten him. Frantically, he wipes and blows at them until they are all off his skin and on the sand. Finally, he places the lid on with great care.

He sits back to look at what he has made, and he is happy, it looks good.

Picking up the instructions, he reads through the steps again to ensure he has done what was needed. 'Wait,' the child says to the emptiness of his room. The printing at the bottom of the instruction sheet has faded so that the seventh step is unreadable. Something is there but he is unable to make it out. He sits back and looks at the farm again. It looks finished, he thinks. With a shrug, he walks over to the blinds and opens them. The sunlight streams in warming the room. He lays down on his stomach in front of the ant farm. With head propped on hands, he watches as the ants clamber over one another. After a time, boredom and hunger overtake him. 'I'll be back soon,' he says to the ants and heads downstairs to the kitchen.

As he descends the stairs, he begins to hear cupboards opening and closing, pots rattling against one another. 'Mum,' he says as he enters the kitchen, 'I didn't hear you get up.' She is still in her nightgown, which hugs her thin frame tight, and a cigarette hangs from her mouth limp and unlit.

'Mum, guess what,' the child says

'Mm?'

'Dad got me an ant farm! Did he bring it into my room? Is he here?'

'Did he, now? Don't ask me how it got there. I haven't seen your father. But he has that key of his so he can come and go as he likes. I should damn well take that off him.'

The boy shrugs. 'Quick, come upstairs and look. You'll love it!' He reaches for her hand, but she moves abruptly, turning away from him to the fridge.

'Later,' she says as she leans into the fridge. 'I need to get your damned lunch ready.' From the fridge she pulls a leg of lamb and some potatoes.

'Wow, Mum. Roast? Are we having roast? We never have roast!'

'Yes, we're having roast,' she says. 'So don't expect any presents from me. This meat cost an arm and a leg.' The child moves to her and hugs her around the waist. 'Okay, happy birthday. Now go get yourself some breakfast and stay out of my way.'

'Where's Dad? When will he get here?' the boy asks as he sets his way about getting breakfast. A pot slams onto the bench, startling him. He turns to see his mother staring at him with brow knitted and arms crossed.

'Please stop asking me that. That's all I've heard for days now. I don't know where your bloody father is. He said he'd be here to help with lunch. But he's not here now, that's for bloody sure. He never is.' She picks up her drink, glass rattles against its edges. 'I wouldn't be surprised if your father doesn't bloody come today. I really wouldn't be.' She rattles the ice around in the bottom of the glass.

'But you said that he'd be here.' Tears begin to fill the boy's eyes.

'Oh, god, don't start crying,' she says. The child

reaches out his arms to her. 'I'm too busy to hug you, can't you see? Let me get this damned lunch cooked for you. Take your breakfast to your room and stay out of the kitchen.'

The child picks up his bowl of cereal and heads upstairs. He hears the ice rattling against the glass again, followed by the distinct sound of the glass being refilled.

~

The ants have begun to create a system of tunnels in the sand. That was quick, the boy thinks as he sits cross-legged on the floor eating his breakfast. He watches with wonder as they work their way through the tunnels, slowly going deeper, digging smaller tunnels leading to large antechambers. The ants' movements are a mystery to him. What are they doing? What are they building? He does not know. The ants are slaves to some deeply instinctual pattern that will remain a mystery to the child. He knows this though; he will love them. He will tend to them, provide food and safety for them. They will never know neglect.

From downstairs, he hears his mother in the kitchen. Her movements come in staccato patterns with thumps and tumbling dishes. And then a broken glass. He ventures back down the stairs and into the kitchen to help, but he is met with a fiery gaze and pointed finger. 'Get back to your bloody room. Can't you see that there's glass here, you silly thing?' The sound of bubbling water fills the air.

'I can help,' the boy says and moves to step into the

kitchen. His mother's eyes halt him. The bubbling crescendos with violence, cracking and spitting, and then silences. Smoke begins to fill the air.

'Mum, the pot!'

The mother looks at the smoke rising from the pot, turns her eyes skyward and curses. As she rises, she grabs a tea towel from the bench and wraps it around her hand, picks the pot up and hurls it into the sink. She turns on the cold water and the pot hisses as it cools.

She turns to the child, 'You and your bloody birthday lunch. Go,' she says. 'Get out of here! Get back to your room!

Tears again begin to fill his eyes as he backs towards the stairs. Back in his room, he lies on the bed, face buried in the pillow.

There are nights where his mother will enter his room in the dark with kindness on her lips. Her kisses and sour breath caress his neck and face as she implores him to wake. There are tears and apologies and promises, even times where she pleads for his help. Through it all, he keeps his eyes closed and breathing steady. After a time, she inevitably walks on unsure feet to her room and falls on the bed into darkness. Sometimes the boy goes into her room to place a blanket over her, but more often he pulls the covers over his head and tightens his body into a ball. Where his father is through all this, he does not know.

~

The boy lifts his head from the pillow. He has been

sleeping and the sun now hangs high in the sky. The house is silent except for the gentle sounds of the wind outside.

He carries the ant farm through to the kitchen. On the counter the potatoes lay untouched and portions of fat cut from the meat attract flies. The heat coming from the oven is oppressive and he is happy to get to the darkened cool of the lounge room.

His mother is sitting in her armchair. The blinds are closed, making it difficult to see. 'Mum?' the boy says. She strikes her lighter, the flame illuminating her face, and lights her cigarette. The flame disappears and the room begins to fill with thick acrid smoke.

'Look,' he says, holding up the ant farm, 'I thought you'd like to see.' She is looking away from him, steadily smoking her cigarette. 'Mum, see? Look.'

She turns to him. 'Mm.'

'Can you see? I did it all myself. I followed the instructions. Well, I tried. I couldn't read the last one, but I think it's done. See?'

'Mm-hm.'

'Mum? Can you see what Dad got me? Can you see what I've made? Can you see the ants?'

An exasperated sigh. 'Yes, goddamnit! I see it. I see what your father got you. I bloody see it!' She picks up her drink and takes a long swallow.

The child puts down the ant farm and moves towards her. 'Mum, it's okay.'

'It's okay? It's *okay?* she says. 'It's okay, you say. What do you know? You don't know, you don't. It's not okay. Here we are in this shithole and he's not here. He's never here! He's out there flogging that damned book of his. Like anyone should care what he has to say.' She drags on her cigarette. 'Do you know what he did after he gave me you? Left. Gone as quick as he came. Sure, he comes back now and then. Whoopty-fucking-doo. What a miracle. He said he'd be here to help me with the lunch. Yeah, right. Why'd I believe that? Should've never given him that damn key. I hope he doesn't come today. I hope he doesn't so you can see what he's really like.' She shields her eyes with her hand as she begins to cry. Through sobs, she keeps on smoking.

'Mum,' the child says, but she does not look at him. 'Mum?' He reaches out to touch her. She swats at his hand, the cigarette ash burning his fingers. The boy draws his hand into himself, head bowed, burnt fingers in his mouth.

'Oh, Jesus! Let me look,' the mother says. He remains still. 'I said, let me look!' She grabs him by the wrist, trying to pull him to her. He resists.

Moaning, tears begin to roll down his cheeks. 'Oh, goddamnit,' she says. 'Go back upstairs if you are going to cry like a baby. Go on! Go! Just go!'

He picks up the ant farm and heads back upstairs. Back in his room, he hears loud footsteps from below, a glass break, a door slam, and then the house is silent.

He puts the ant farm on the nightstand and sits on the bed. The ants, oblivious to him, continue with their digging. The boy wonders what it would be like to be one of them, whether he would be accepted, whether he would have the strength to dig and dig and dig until the job was done. He picks up the birthday card and reads it again, *For you, my son. Dad.* He has not seen his father for some time. The last time was fleeting, a quick hug and hello and then his father was gone again. But he had promised to be here today for a birthday lunch and the boy had held onto that promise tightly.

There is a commotion downstairs. The boy opens his bedroom door and listens. *Dad,* he thinks. 'It's Dad,' he says to the ants. 'It's my Dad, he's here! I can't wait to show you to him. Wait here and I'll bring him up.'

The boy bounds down the stairs, but as he reaches the bottom he hears yelling.

'I said I'd be here, didn't I? And here I am.'

'Late,' the boy's mother says, 'Late as always. You said you'd be here to help with the lunch. But instead all I got were pots of water boil dry and potatoes left unpeeled and uncut!'

The boy stands at the doorway. His father says, 'Well, you could've done that yourself. You don't need me for that. But you probably just sat around with a drink.'

'Fuck you,' the mother says. 'Fuck you and the high horse you rode in on. Such a big, important man. Bullshit. I know you. I *know* you.'

'Here!' The father grabs the pot from the sink and fills it with water, lights a burner on the stovetop and sits the pot atop the flame. 'There! Happy? Water boiling.'

'Get out. Go. Just go! We don't need you!'

'No,' the boy screams. Man and woman turn to face him. 'You can't, you can't go Dad! Mum! Please let him stay.'

The father tries to hug the son but the mother steps between them. 'No. You don't get to have him after all this time.' The boy is crying. 'Get out! Get out you piece of shit!'

'Fine, you want me gone? I'll go!' The boy's father starts for the front door.

'No! Dad, wait! Please. Let me show you the ant farm.'

His father stops and smiles. 'Quick.'

The boy races from the kitchen to his room, taking the stairs two at a time. He grabs the ant farm from his room and starts back down the stairs with care. The boy holds the ant farm up for his father to see.

'You've done well,' the father says. 'Did you follow all the instructions?'

Before the boy can answer his mother shouts, 'Oh, shit! The meat! The bloody meat!' Smoke is starting to rise from the oven. His mother opens the oven door and from the smoky depths pulls the charred remains of their meal. 'Jesus-fucking-Christ,' she spits the words out between clenched teeth. As the boy holds up the ant farm for his father to see his mother throws the meat and tray to the ground in a fury. The tray knocks the ant farm from the boy's hands and it all smashes against the floor, meat and sand and ants crashing in a chaotic mess. The child looks at his mother and then at the shattered farm and then at his father. Tears begin to fill his eyes. 'The ants! The bloody ants!' the mother screams as ants begin to spread out across the kitchen. The father pushes the son out of the way, pulls the now boiling pot of water from the stovetop and dumps it over the ants. The mother's and the boy's wailing fill the kitchen.

The father tries to soothe both the mother and the son. 'It's okay, it's okay you two,' he says. I'll get more meat, I'll get another ant farm. It's okay, calm down. I can fix this.' The boy watches as his father moves to hug his mother. She resists at first, beating at his chest with clenched fists, but seeing the boy kneeling before them, hands upturned, eyes awash with tears, she relents and allows the father to take her in his arms.

'I'm so sick of this, so sick of it,' she sobs into the sturdy chest of her once betrothed. 'Why me? Why? I'm so tired. Take it away. Take it all away.'

The boy cries as he watches the scene before him, the ants floating dead in the water. He starts to suck on his thumb.

The father, holding the mother as she cries, studies the child with contemplation. It has not been a good day. Through tear-filled eyes, the boy watches as his father leans his head down to his mother's ear, eyes still fixed on him, studying him as he weeps. His father speaks to his mother: **'There, there,' he whispers in her ear. 'There, there. It will soon be over.'**[8]

---

[8] Last line from *The Lives of Animals*, J M Coetzee

House Auctions

Bala Mudaly

Auctions are a nightmare for new migrants. It certainly was for my wife and me when we went househunting thirty years ago. In my experience, houses were always advertised in the papers under the 'Properties for Sale' columns. At least this was how it was done in South Africa. We'd never experienced auctions until we set foot here.

On our arrival in Australia in 1988, we lived in Elsternwick with a relative of my wife's, Auntie Jay, also an ex-South African. A gesture of temporary goodwill. Most migrants need a leg-up to make it in a new country.

'Yeah, that's it, Hashim. It's how houses are sold here. Auctioned,' Auntie Jay said.

'Really?'

'In fact, two houses in our street are up for auction in a fortnight. You must have seen the auction boards.'

'No, haven't paid much attention. Jet lag and all that.'

'But surely you can't not have seen them. Large, and almost in your face with airbrushed photos of the property.'

Auntie Jay was eager to help. And for our part, we did not wish to overstretch her hospitality.

'I'll take you both to the auctions. But you'll be interested to see the houses before then when they're open for inspection.'

'Eh?'

Auntie Jay explained how in the weeks before the auction, houses were prepared for inspection by prospective buyers.

~

In two months we'd made some progress settling in. My wife was already in a reasonably well-paying job, and I'd lined up a few promising interviews. It was time to take on the next challenge: buying a house.

Having already attended a few auctions, we now had some idea of how it worked. But we still lacked confidence. Even visualising ourselves, out there, actually bidding, was enough to give me the jitters. Auntie Jay coaxed us with a reassuring step-by-step strategy—first scan the auction pages in the Friday issue of the Melbourne *Age*, highlight a few houses in Ormond, Bentleigh and Glen Huntly—suburbs close to family support. And then check them out before the auction.

'Oh, thanks. That certainly helps. Is that it?'

'No, no. You'll have to work out how big a house will suit you—bedrooms, garage, single or double-storey, big or small back yard. You know, things like that. But also, what you can afford.'

'My god, it's now getting complicated,' my wife said with a sigh, draining the last drop from her water bottle.

'And that's not all,' continued Auntie Jay, like she relished inflicting pain. 'Houses away from high-traffic roads, closer to parks, schools, shops and public transport, cost more. Much more. Even beyond what the bank may loan you.'

~

We had a few sleepless nights before fronting up to bid for the first house that struck our fancy and had passed our *tick-box* test.

'Look at the kitchen, dear. Clean and neat. Even has a dishwasher. You do know domestic help is unheard of here. Not like in Durban.'

'Not so loud, Deb,' I whispered, a little sensitive to prospective buyers nearby, opening and closing cupboards.

~

I recall us elbowing past a throng of people in the passageway, just before the auction was to commence. It had three smallish bedrooms, two with built-in wardrobes, plus a new kitchen. What's more, it was near a train station and a respectable shopping strip. What else would we need?

'But wait,' Auntie Jay said, all starry-eyed. 'Just think, you'll be a stone's throw from Chaddy.'

'Chaddy, what's Chaddy?'

'Oops sorry. Forgot you're new here.'

'Well?'

'Chadstone is a mega shopping complex. Some say largest in the southern hemisphere.'

'Wow, Hashim, then we must get this house,' my wife said with a determined look.

Yeah, at all cost, I thought.

~

Presently we were all ushered to the front of the house for the auction. Fortunately, the sun was out. It was warm and cheerful. The crowd closed in and faced the auctioneer, a jaunty man of about forty, full of himself; slick from head to toe—clean-cut face, plastered hair, dark suit, red tie and shiny pointy shoes. Black. I thought it interesting how estate agents, politicians, financial planners and insurance brokers seem to be made from the same mould—a fast-talking class of their own.

People stood all over the place, on the pavements and nature-strips—men and women, a few kids, a passive black Labrador next to a wriggling child in a pram. Everyone seemed expectant yet a little nervous, shifting on their feet and looking away from the auctioneer, who had a rolled-up wad of paper in his right hand. He scanned the crowd with a practised eye before rattling off the rules of the auction and then highlighting the assets of the property on offer.

In the meantime, two of his team moved among the crowd. They showed particular interest in two Asian couples who had turned up. Once the auction was in progress, the agents seemed to egg them to stay ahead of other bids. I found this quite annoying.

It was not surprising then that we lost this house, even without raising a finger. It sold for what we thought was a preposterous sum. So, you would guess how devastated we felt when the possibility of owning this house also popped like a bubble as the auctioneer struck the rolled-up paper for a third and decisive time. Within minutes, the chatting crowd shifted and dispersed, leaving us stranded and wondering what next. A middle-aged woman with a gaudy perm, fancy sunglasses and a bulging Emilio Masi bag disappeared into the house with the auctioneer.

~

Gloom and despair took over. The little confidence we'd had, evaporated. We couldn't imagine ourselves ever winning in this mindless auction game. But we soldiered on.

~

Here am I now, years later, often driving past the dream house that we lost, resisting an urge to pull over and inspect it yet again. I smile wryly. How ironic that I should now feel convinced it would have been an absolutely bad buy. How perceptions shift with time and circumstances. The truth is that desperation to own a house had blunted our judgement then. How could we have even considered this property a good enough option?

I marvel at how hideous it looks, squatting there like a bullfrog, partially hidden behind a couple of gums. The front yard is narrow and neglected. Four pillars support the front gable over an L-shaped veranda, pillars that remind me of the stumpy legs of a hippo. Yes, that's it, a squatting bullfrog with ungainly hippo legs. How bizarre! Moreover, it is a weatherboard house, over fifty years old I'd say, on noisy Glen Huntly Road. The colours of the exterior walls are revolting—industrial green on the verandah and the rest of the walls a shitty ochre. Oh well, there's no accounting for people's tastes.

~

September slipped by taking its cue from July and August. I was still without a job. Auntie Jay made as if she was caught in much busyness, leaving us alone with the burden of finding a place to live. Perhaps she'd be thinking: 'I did my bit showing them the ropes. It's up to them now how they sort themselves out.' Apart from casually mentioning one day that she was expecting visitors from South Africa over Christmas, she rarely now enquired what luck we were having in househunting. The atmosphere had become decidedly cool. We felt the pressure and regretted migrating to Australia.

~

There was no turning back now. The only option was to keep at it. The Sunday Melbourne *Age* usually listed the houses auctioned and sold on the previous day, or if they were passed in. I was beginning to understand how the housing market worked. We also routinely checked the houses for sale and auction columns in this edition. The listings were generally sparse when compared with that in the Friday's *Age*.

On the second Sunday of November, we decided to check out a house in Hughesdale. It was open for inspection and was to be auctioned in a fortnight's time. When borrowing Auntie Jay's car, we mentioned that we were headed to inspect a property in Hughesdale.

'But why so far?' she queried.

'Oh, we heard the houses there were more affordable,' I explained wondering why she thought it was too far.

In any case, we drove slowly up the street in Hughesdale looking for the house in question. Paperbark trees lined the nature strip on either side of the road. Not too many cars parked along the kerb. I pulled up beside the 'For Auction' board on my side.

'No that can't be right,' said my wife who had the *Age* in her hand and was reading off the street numbers. 'It says 17, but we've stopped at number 11.'

I glanced at the newspaper. 'Yeah, No, 11's not even listed. That's strange.'

We got out and stood scanning the noticeboard. Then took in the property. The house was a 1950s weatherboard, in reasonably good condition—at least on the outside. Nothing fancy. A jacaranda tree with an expansive canopy graced the front garden. Sitting underneath on a well-tendered lawn was a wheelbarrow converted to a flowerbox, now overflowing with pink and purple petunias in full bloom. A single white butterfly flitted about. Along the perimeters of the garden were upright wooden trellises which supported sweet peas, in a riot of colours. What an impressive show on a bright summer's day!

'You interested in our house?' It was an elderly woman who appeared from the side of the building, with a green watering can. A small energetic woman with an apron over a loose floral dress, floppy hat, runners and gardening gloves. She smiled and the creases of her aged face reflected her delight.

'Sorry,' I said, feeling a little flustered. 'No, no, just looking. Hope it's okay?'

'It will be in the papers next Saturday.'

'Oh, thanks,' said Deb. 'That explains it.'

The lady put down her can and removed her hat revealing a dishevelled white fluff.

She wiped her brow on the sleeve of her overall. 'Predict a scorcher today,' she said taking a step towards us, a knee-height picket fence separating us.

'Where you from—India? All us folk in this street are born Aussies. Mostly built our own houses.'

A warm breeze stirred in the jacaranda.

'When'll your house be open for inspection?' queried Deb.

'Oh, you could come in now if you wish. Meet Mal, my husband. He'll be keen to show you the place.'

I glanced at my wife to see if she was as taken aback as I was with the spontaneous invitation.

'Thanks, but we don't wish to intrude on your privacy. Especially on a Sunday,' said Deb.

'No, no, no worries. Give me a sec while I open the gate. Come in and I'll get something to cool you down. Mind the sun. Simply bad, you know.'

The house felt much cooler than outside. With windows shuttered and curtains drawn, the dim lighting seemed to add to the cooling effect.

An elderly man with a smooth cheerful face and a comfortable paunch waddled into the living room, bare feet, singlet and black track pants. His thinning hair was plastered back, adding to his broad forehead.

Hello, hello and who have we here, Marge?

'Folks looking for a house. Show them around, dear.'

Marge apologised for not introducing herself earlier. We told them our names and a little of who we were. While Marge got us drinks, Mal painted us a picture of his life story which it appeared was tied up intimately with this house and his long marriage to Marge. He pointed to photos on the shelf above the fireplace saying his two daughters were born here and have since grown into adults and set themselves up in life. No grandchildren as yet. 'But,' he added with a wistful look, 'one can't have everything in life.'

In half an hour, Deb and I felt strangely at home, as if we belonged to this house. Marge and Mal had so warmed to us, that they seemed quite in earnest to entrust their house to us, the place in which they had invested almost their entire adult lives.

They pointed out things they'd leave behind for the new owners, items they'd not need or accommodate in their one-room unit at Happy Valley Retirement Village. The items included a wall unit with a selection of drink glasses, a kitchen table and chairs, garden furniture, and two well-used cane chairs installed side-by-side in the fernery, with a panoramic view of a thriving back garden. Marge explained they'd especially miss the chairs because this was where they'd sat with their breakfast, lunch and dinners all through many, many summers. Such a loss. 'But not to worry,' she said with a laugh. They'd not be leaving behind their memories for the next occupants. That would be giving away far too much.

So it was that we came to live in Hughesdale, thirty years ago. The house was withdrawn from auction and sold to us at a bargain-basement price. Auntie Jay fell off her chair when told.

'Your colour didn't matter to them? That's truly remarkable.'

We kept in touch with both Mal and Marge until the very end. **They knew where they were going, smiling at death in the shade of a ghost-gum.**[9]

---

[9] Last line from *The Songlines*, Bruce Chatwin

Synchronicity

Robert New

Sitting at his kitchen bench, on a four-legged barstool, Matthew Lexum sipped his morning coffee appreciatively. He spread the Saturday paper over the grey stone benchtop. As was his custom, he started with the job ads. His current manager, Neil, was horribly out of his depth and took his fear of being found out, out on his team. Matthew couldn't understand how it was Neil couldn't understand the basics of sales. They were flogging used vehicles. It wasn't rocket science. Matthew had been the leading salesperson for years and knew the business inside and out. He'd never wanted a promotion, but if he was offered Neil's job, he'd take it just to get rid of the man.

The first ad he saw was a huge, half-page spread advertising a job at Synchronicity. The company sold what it billed as 'esoteric life improvement services'. Very little was in the public domain about what they did. They were as secretive as a religion founded by a sci-fi author. It was known the cost of their basic package was a cool quarter of a million dollars. They'd be great to work for. He might even get to meet some of their celebrity endorsers. Both of the latest Oscar-winning actors, the Best Picture director, and the Time 'Person of the Year' had each thanked the company in their speeches. They'd described the services as life-changing and said they never knew how rich life could be before using Synchronicity. No wonder they were looking for a new salesperson, all the wealthy elite wanted in.

Matthew called his German Shepard, who dutifully trotted over and sat next to him. 'Good girl, Ruby,' Mathew said as he reached down and scratched her ears. He looked Ruby in the eye and sighed. 'What should I do, Ruby-Lou? D'you think I should apply?'

Ruby tilted her head sideways and looked at Matthew earnestly. 'You're right. To go from selling cars to that would be a bridge too far. Plus, what if it meant I wouldn't be home in time to take you walkies each evening?'

At the mention of the keyword, Ruby stood and whined excitedly. 'Okay, Okay. My fault for saying it. Let's go walkies.'

Ruby began hopping in circles, then ran to get her lead from by the front door. A moment later she returned with it in her mouth. Matthew slurped the last of his coffee and took the lead. He felt a smile creep onto his face. Ruby's uncomplicated enthusiasm for little things always made Matthew happier.

~

The local dog park was a short stroll around the corner from his home. He'd just thrown the ball for Ruby, using a ball thrower, when his phone rang. It was an unlisted number. Matthew answered, expecting it to be telemarketers, he spoke gruffly, 'Whaddya want?'

'Hello, Mr Lexum. Sorry for interrupting your weekend.' The voice sounded like it belonged to a member of the British upper class. Matthew stopped walking towards Ruby who had started running towards him after retrieving the ball.

'Uh, yeah. That's okay. Who is this?'

'My name is Johnson Alcove. I'm part of a small team and my company has asked me to see if you'd be interested in joining our salesforce. Are you currently looking for a new employer?'

'Yes, I guess I am. But, may I ask who you work for?'

'Synchronicity.'

'Get outta here. I was just looking at their ad in the paper.' Matthew barely noticed Ruby drop the ball at his feet.

'Excellent. I know it's an odd request, but could you please come to our city office tomorrow morning at nine? Head for the underground car park off Lafurl Lane. Someone will guide you to a parking spot. At reception ask for me, Johnson Alcove, and they'll show you up.'

Normally Sundays were when Matthew made the most sales at work, but the dealership was closed for a long weekend. It was like it was meant to be.

'I can make that.'

'Wonderful. I look forward to meeting you then. Enjoy the rest of your Saturday.'

'Will do.'

Ruby whined and looked from the ball to Matthew and back.

Matthew watched her repeat the action with a sense of unreality. Had that call just happened? He checked the call log to see. Yep, definitely a call from an unknown number.

~

Matthew spent most of the day researching Synchronicity. Unfortunately, he couldn't find out much more than he already knew. They were immensely successful almost from the moment they'd started operations. Their founder, Cheswick Lafurl, had become a billionaire within five years, and the company had no real competitors, after all, no one was quite sure what they sold: All their clients and employees were made to sign non-disclosure agreements.

The clients Matthew could establish they'd provided services for were all immensely successful, but it was more than that, they seemed happy and enthusiastic about life. How were Synchronicity achieving it? In a memo purporting to be between members of the organisation Matthew found on WikiLeaks, there was a reference to an acronym CUAR, but no other useful information.

Matthew was frustrated. He'd never gone into a job interview without a clear understanding of the company he was intending to work for.

~

The next morning Matthew checked his appearance in a mirror before he left. His charcoal suit was light enough to not seem too formal, nor too casual. Matthew combed his grey-flecked black hair and checked his nostrils for errant hairs and boogers. He looked good. His dark eyelashes and white sclera accentuated the hazel of his irises, and his lightly tanned skin added an aura of health. It was a carefully cultivated image. One that had been aided by some weight loss and a healthier diet since his wife left two years ago. It still hadn't helped him find a new partner though, but maybe a job change would help him meet some new people?

Matthew drove to the city from his suburban home. The traffic was light, and he cruised in. The sun was rising behind the skyscraper as he approached, and its silhouette was impressively large. Even with the backlight, the large golden letters of 'Synchronicity' were clearly visible at the top of the building. Matthew turned into the laneway beside the building and was directed by a man wearing an official-looking hi-vis vest to a car park near an elevator. The official told Matthew that 'these lifts only go to the foyer. You'll need to check in there.' Matthew remembered the first rule of interviews to treat everyone like they were your new boss, and thanked him appropriately.

The white-glass walls of the lift gave the impression of being ultra-modern, and the reception foyer furthered this by more white-glass walls and a floor covered in metre-squared sized tiles. There was a separate reception desk for Synchronicity compared to the other companies with offices in the building. Combined with discreet gold lettering, the effect was powerful. Here was a company which exerted influence. Their private elevator went straight to Synchronicity's floor. Matthew felt giddy as he stepped into their reception area. His vertigo wasn't helped by the extensive view of the city from the full-length windows.

A smartly dressed woman greeted Matthew and directed him through a maze of corridors to Johnson Alcove's office. Despite it being a Sunday morning, there were quite a few people around. Would he have to work on weekends? Part of the appeal of a new job was that he might get some extra time to spend with his daughter, who lived with his ex-wife. If the money was right, it wouldn't be a deal breaker. Corporate sales sounded a lot better than used-car salesman.

The office rivalled Matthew's living room for size and was in stark contrast to the tiny cubicle he used to write-up sales. Three armchairs were arranged in a triangle. Each had their own side table with water and a coffee already placed on it. Matthew noted the coffee by the vacant chair was a macchiato. His preferred coffee. It wasn't one people would pick for someone else by default. How could they know that? Was it a coincidence?

He took it as a good sign.

Matthew took the chair indicated for him, surprised no one offered to shake hands, nor did Johnson, or the other gentleman beside him, stand to greet their interviewee. It was obvious which was Johnson, as he practically reeked of upper-crust Britain. From his perfectly manicured silver hair and moustache, light blue-grey suit, bow tie and demeanour, it just seemed wrong he wasn't wearing a bowler hat. His middle-aged colleague's suit was equally sharply tailored, and his shirt looked like it had a very high thread count. However, he wasn't wearing a tie. He seemed vaguely familiar, but Matthew couldn't place him, but then again, he'd probably just seen a picture during his research.

'Welcome Matthew, thank you for giving up your Sunday to come in to meet with us. As I said on the phone yesterday, my name is Johnson Alcove,' the British looking man said. 'This is the founder of Synchronicity, Cheswick Lafurl.'

'Pleased to meet you,' Cheswick chimed in before Matthew could say those exact words himself.

'Likewise,' Matthew replied, wishing he'd thought of something stronger to say in response.

'I hear you were looking for a new job and saw our ad in the paper yesterday?' Cheswick queried.

'Yes.'

'And then we phoned asking you for an interview.' Cheswick's eyes were alive with … something? Was that mirth?

'Yes.'

'Seems fortuitous. And then you arrived, and we had your preferred drink ready.' Cheswick replied.

'Yes.' Matthew made sure he spoke the word clearly, without resorting to a 'yeah'. Diction was important in interviews and sales alike.

Cheswick leant forward. 'Let me quote something to you. "When coincidences pile up in this way, one cannot help being impressed by them—for the greater the number of items in such a series, or the more unusual its character, the more improbable it becomes." The man who inspired much of what we do here, Carl Jung, said that. What do you think about it?'

'Seems to fit. I feel like this is where I'm meant to be.'

'We're going to have to pause at this point ...' Johnson said. 'So you can sign a non-disclosure agreement, or NDA as they're commonly called. What we reveal next as part of the interview process is privileged information. Do you understand?'

'Yes. I can't talk about any of it to anyone outside of the company.'

'Good. Please read through the document. We'll just step outside for a couple of minutes while you do so. Just tap on the coffee table beside you when you're ready for us to return. Take your time.'

Matthew started reading through the document as the two gentlemen left the room. It was immediately clear they weren't messing around. The contract explained that any discussion of the methods or services used by

Synchronicity was prohibited. Matthew could identify them as his employer, discuss salary and provisions, but only give the broadest possible explanation for what he would actually be doing if he was successful in applying for the job. One clause seemed interesting. It said to point it out to the interviewers for an immediate cash bonus of $5000. Matthew guessed it was there to see if the person read through the contract fully. Otherwise, the contract seemed as rigid, or even more so, than the one his brother had shown him when he'd applied to ASIO. If Matthew broke the contract, his life would be over.

Matthew swigged the last of his coffee and tapped on the coffee table. A few seconds later Johnson and Cheswick were seated in front of him again.

'So, what do you think?' Cheswick asked.

'It's pretty clear-cut. I guess what it's describing is that you will own a portion of my life and have the right to determine what I can say about it.'

'Correct.'

Matthew took a breath.

'But what's up with clause 24e?'

Cheswick grinned. 'Well spotted. Here is the money.' He reached into his right jacket pocket and handed Matthew a wad of cash.

Matthew tried not to react, but he felt his face flush, suddenly embarrassed by seeming too interested in money. He reached for his water glass to calm his reaction.

'Speaking of which,' Johnson said nonchalantly, 'the

starting salary is three hundred and forty thousand dollars.'

Matthew dropped the glass of water. Fortunately, he'd only just lifted it off its coaster. It clinked as it fell back into place, but didn't tip over. The salary was about four times what he was earning now.

'No one pays that kind of money for sales. What will I be doing?'

'Sales. But you need to understand what we do, in order to understand why our salary offer is so high. It's all legal, in case that needs to be said, but the ethics of it can … uh … confuse some applicants for our sales jobs. Can you sign the NDA please?' Cheswick asked.

Matthew nodded. What on earth was he getting into? Once he'd signed the form, he gave it to Cheswick who pulled a pair of reading glasses from his left jacket pocket and put them on. It was then that Matthew recognised him.

'Hang on. Did I sell you a car a couple of months ago?'

Cheswick grinned as he signed the form. 'Yes. Now, can you tell me what we discussed during the sales process?'

Matthew thought back to the sale. It was hard to remember everyone who bought a car from him, let alone who came through the dealership.

'I'm not sure.'

'Well let me remind you of how you sold me on the car. It was a similar strategy to what we like our sales team to use. You made me affirm it was time for me to upgrade my car, sold me on the features of the vehicle and allowed me to take a long, unaccompanied drive in it, something your fellow salespeople didn't offer when I spoke to them earlier in the week. Then when I returned you made a time-limited deal, so it would appear like I had to buy it straight away.'

'Sure. That sounds like me. It's a simple formula, fix the need, develop the taste, buy the product or get laid to waste.'

'Then when it came to negotiating the price you never wavered on the dollar amount, only on the inclusions. Why was that?'

'All the low-balling, door-in-face, foot-in-door sales practices tend to make a person feel good about the sale, but not as good about me. I've found when I keep the price fixed, I get more referrals from customers since they see me as a straight-shooter.'

Both Cheswick and Johnson smiled.

'You also said something about how employees leave managers, not companies when I coaxed your poachability out of you.'

'That's right,' Matthew said as more of their conversation came back to him.

'You gave the distinct impression of someone who was thinking about looking further afield for new employment opportunities. I suggested you read the Saturday paper for the job ads, as I'd heard some new sales jobs would be advertised in a few weeks.'

'I remember now. Actually, that was what started my search. Hey, you even commented on my choice of coffee.'

'And then you received a paper yesterday morning with our ad. Did you know that the ad was only in your copy? It doesn't take much to switch the one on your driveway when you get it delivered.

Matthew felt the confusion show on his face.

'We couldn't be sure when you'd read it, so we waited until we saw you take your dog for a walk, guessing you'd have read the paper before going out. So, tell us. Now you know what we did to make you feel a sense of destiny, a sense of being in the right place at the right time, does it diminish the effect?'

Matthew wished he could avoid the question, but they were waiting on his answer. 'I guess not. I mean in a nutshell, it's amazing someone would go to such effort to make me feel like that, even if the effect was only small.'

'Well, that is what we sell. We make our clients feel like things around them are happening just for them. Your experience was nothing compared to what we do for our clients. Let me give you some detail about our history.'

Matthew's sense of unreality left him with no choice but to agree.

~

'When I was just a run-of-the-mill concierge, I occasionally met famous people. After a time, I became less starstruck when dealing with them, and over time came to realise many were normal people who sought fame, and who, having found it, were afraid of how shallow and superficial life was for them. Most didn't feel like they deserved their fame once they'd earnt it, which just fed into their anxieties. One day I was behind the desk with not much to do, so I went to an online encyclopedia and asked it for a random page. What it returned was about an inherited thing called the collective unconscious. I hadn't heard of it before so found the idea intriguing. Put simply, it's a system of archetypal symbols which people give meaning to by relating them to their experiences. This concept led Jung to develop the idea of synchronicity—the idea that just as events may be connected by a cause and effect relationship, they may also be connected by meaning. For example, there is a story told about Jung treating a patient who'd been dreaming of a golden scarab. Right as she was telling Jung about this, there was the noise of something banging at the window. Jung went over and found a golden beetle which he let in and held in his hands as he returned to his patient. He presented it to her with the words "and here is your scarab". After that, the patient stopped trying to be purely rational and accept a more human explanation of behaviour. Are you following?'

'Yes, I think so. The beetle was a coincidence, but it's meaning for the patient was something greater because she related it to her dream,' Matthew said.

'Excellent. Meaning is very important in all of this. We relate it to the collective unconsciousness and acausal relationships.'

Matthew recognised the CUAR acronym he'd read about.

'Anyway, later that afternoon after I'd read about it, I was talking to a new guest of the hotel. I mentioned my interest in psychology and they immediately started talking about Jung. I had previously only heard of him in passing, and never read about synchronicity or the collective unconscious before that morning, yet here I was having a detailed conversation about them, not two hours after first hearing of the ideas. This made the concepts seem powerful and got me thinking how by looking for a few such coincidences in one's life, you could feel a connection to humanity which would be life-affirming. You'd feel like life had a rhythmic pulse to it.'

'Why do you target celebrities?' Matthew asked.

Cheswick smiled. 'It's not simply celebrities, it's actors. When I was a concierge, the ones I met were so obsessed with every review, every whisper amongst their colleagues. They were so desperate to feel special and worthy of what came their way. They were the perfect target for this program. Plus, the successful ones, which are the only ones we work with, have more money than they know what to do with, yet no meaning in their lives. It just added up. That's why we charge so much. Not only do we want to earn a lot of money, when it costs as much as we charge, the celebrities ascribe more meaning to it. If we charged only one thousand, they wouldn't expect much and not much would change for them. Charge at least a quarter mill', and they make things change for themselves. We do, however, go to some extent to set-up coincidences for them to notice. Part of your job would be doing that.'

Johnson leant forward as Cheswick paused to take a sip of his coffee. 'You were surprised by our salary offer to you. You shouldn't be. We tell clients we cater for five hundred clients at a time. That's an arbitrary number we chose when we started to further imply exclusivity, not a real limit. We do reject clients who we see as being less susceptible to our methods. But on average our clients spend just over half a million per annum with us and, currently, we have six hundred and forty-three. We set up a lot of coincidences for them in their first few months of membership, then decrease the frequency. By the time they've reached their third year with us, we're not actually doing anything for them. We just use cold reading techniques to make them think we're behind certain events in their life.'

Matthew did a quick mental calculation. The numbers were extraordinary. That amount of revenue versus operating costs. No wonder they could pay him so much.

'Which is why it's only a starting salary. If you keep our clients happy and signed up, you'll triple that within three years.'

Matthew exhaled, nearly whistling as he did so.

'How long will your current employer need?'

'Four weeks is what they say is preferred, but our agreement actually says two weeks is all that's required.

I've read through it.' Matthew grinned.

'Your manager will be a woman, named Lacey Wittner. Are you okay with working for a woman?'

Matthew jumped. Lacey was his high-school crush, not that he'd ever told her. Since when was she working here? What were the odds?

'Fine with working for a woman, but I know her.'

'Do you?' Cheswick glanced at Johnson. Ever so briefly their faces betrayed their surprise. Almost immediately, both gave a slowly formed smile.

Cheswick leaned forward again. 'One of the sales lines we usually spout, is something along the lines of, in a thousand independent trials, the probability of an event with a 99.9% chance of *not* happening, taking place at least once, is 63.2%. Low probability doesn't have to mean rarely occurring.'

'It's okay, I can work with her. But are you sure you haven't tapped into something real? I mean, seriously, I've wanted to get in touch with her for years. Then all the things which had to happen to bring me here did so. It's quite the chain of events … Synchronicity is an easy thing to sell isn't it?'

'Yes,' Johnson replied.

'There's just one thing I don't get,' Matthew said.

'What's that?' Johnson said.

'Well if all the meaning is in the eye of the beholder and they could just as easily look for such things without us, then are we really selling anything at all? Isn't it all bullshit?'

Cheswick looked at Johnson, who nodded, then back to Matthew.

'Yes. Which leads us to the question. Are you okay with that?'

'Excuse me?' Matthew just managed to avoid saying 'Huh?'

'We know it's all bullshit, as you phrased it, but it makes us a ton of money. We'd like to offer you the job of selling our program to people. You know the salary. It's a forty-hour week, where you get to manage the time those hours occur, and some evenings and travel will be needed, but you have to be committed to what you do. An insincere salesman is of no use to us. So, can you cast aside any ethical concerns and join us?'

Matthew thought about walking into the dealership on Tuesday and how satisfying it would be to tell Neil he was quitting. That had an appeal, but ultimately it was thoughts of Ruby which swayed the decision. Her excitement for little things was something he'd be helping humans to achieve. Even if it was coming from a disingenuous place, wouldn't the ends justify the means? Maybe he should look for such things in his life, himself? After all, how many times had he told himself bad luck comes in threes, so after breaking a shoelace and spilling a coffee in the morning, had he looked for, and found, a third case of bad luck? It was the same principle. The events had no cause and effect relationship, it was the meaning he applied which made them connected. What was wrong with selling a positive version of that?

'Yes, I can. I'd love to be a salesman for you.'

'Welcome aboard. We'll see you here on the … 21st then. Park as you did before and we'll start your orientation.'

This time, they all shook hands as Matthew left.

~

When Matthew arrived home, Ruby greeted him enthusiastically, running around him in circles and pawing at him. Matthew stayed still and let her work off her energy while he contemplated how his life was about to change. **He stood there, like that, for a long time.**[10]

---

[10] Last line from *The Dark Half*, Stephen King

From Time to Time

Andy Russell

Wilbur examined the bearded face peering back at him from the mirror and pulled his coarse woollen cap firmly into place.

'Perfect.'

He checked; drinking gourd full, and woven reed satchel with a meal of unremarkable bread and cheese. The pouch held a few bronze and silver coins and tucked into his waistband a handmade knife with its smooth bone handle. They wouldn't look out of place. What might draw attention was the elegant gold bracelet he added to the leather pouch. With a smile he imagined the look of delight as he offered it to the woman who occupied his thoughts and dreams. His hands trembled with excitement. This was it – the point of no return – he tapped the control panel of the time-transporter to open the door and then pressed his palm against a hidden switch to close it behind him. A blast of bitterly cold, damp air couldn't diminish his enthusiasm. Pulling the fur-lined cloak close around his neck, he strode off into the gathering gloom without a backward glance.

~

Marcia made a show of scooping half a ladle of broth into the rough wooden bowl.

'That's all you're getting, you good for nothing parasite.' For emphasis, she waved her ladle at the hunched, pitiful figure.

Now, Feran was forced to survive on charity, and Marcia was becoming less charitable with each passing day. She made no attempt to conceal her contempt. Things had been different before his eyesight began to fail. In those days, he could turn his hand to any metalworking task the Roman garrison required and was well paid for his work. Every day he cursed the bad luck which had robbed him of his sight, his friends and prospects of raising a family.

'Thank you kindly Marcia and may the gods reward your generosity.'

Feran bowed deeply and stumbled away, choosing a less prominent spot where there was still some benefit from the fire. Huddling down against the wind driven rain he cupped the bowl with both hands to make the most of its dwindling warmth. The thin liquid tasted of rabbit with a few vegetable pieces. He was almost fainting with hunger and the broth together with a stolen hunk of bread would be his only food for the day.

Later in the evening, he sensed a change of

atmosphere around the fire.   The murmur of conversation between casual labourers and other camp followers died to an uneasy silence. Plagued by poor eyesight, he could, at best, make out the fire and people gathered around as flickering shadows. However, he was sure Tolan, the fort commander's underling, had arrived on his nightly rounds. He enjoyed demonstrating his authority by tormenting the outcasts dependant on the commander's charity. Heat from the fire was cut off as he towered over the crouching figure. The wind carried an aroma of hops to Feran's nose made acutely sensitive by hunger.

'You still here worm? By Jupiter, I've told you before, leave, before I flay your sorry hide.'

A blow from a vine stick spun the bowl from Feran's fingers. Following impacts rained down on his legs and arms. Turning to offer his back to the onslaught, he levered himself upright with the support of his staff. Tolan changed to kicks and prods, shepherding his victim towards the path leading away from the fort.

'But, it's too dark to make out the way.'

'Well, it's your fault. You should've gone long ago.'

With a final shove, he sent his victim staggering down the hill and stood watching to make sure there was no turning back. At first, it was easy to follow the path but soon the ground became uneven and bushes tugged at his clothing. No longer on the path, he was lost. Looking around there were no signs of the torches or fires around the fort. The rain had increased to a steady downpour soaking through his torn and patched rags. The cast-off and often repaired leather shoes were no match for the mud. He had a terrible realisation of the hopelessness of his situation. Without shelter, he wouldn't survive the night.

Feran had always been dismissive of the gods worshiped by his parents but staggering deeper into the forest his mind turned to barely remembered prayers and invocations. Perhaps giving insufficient attention to his footing, a tree root snagged his ankle and he landed heavily. Winded and disoriented, he sat in the mud and massaged his knees. Without any idea of the way to the village, there seemed little point in trying to go any further.

At first, he thought it was an illusion. In the distance, barely visible, was a wavering glimmer of light. Feran's heart skipped a beat. Any light must mean help and shelter. Crawling forward, he became increasingly puzzled. It appeared like the door to a brightly lit room repeatedly opening and closing. Uncertain, he watched as the door continued to open wide and then smoothly close until almost totally shut. Once again, he cursed his failing eyesight. Now, when he really needed to see what was going on, he couldn't. A sudden heavy squall helped make a decision. As the opening reached its maximum, he crawled inside.

Even though the door never fully closed, the space inside was dry and warm. By touch, he located a place to sit, and using the clearer edges of his field of view examined his surroundings. There were many brightly coloured shapes on the wall in front of him. On the floor, a tree branch seemed to be jammed in the door and this was why it failed to close properly. Everything else was a mystery, but this was easy to understand. He kicked the branch away and the door closed completely and stayed shut. After sitting totally still for a few minutes appreciating the warmth, his curiosity drove him to explore the patches of colour with his fingers. Some were smooth and others a little raised. He was alarmed when a loud voice spoke a few words in an incomprehensible language. There was no one else in the room. After recovering from the surprise, he pressed the red patch again. A loud trumpet blast sounded three times and all went dark.

~

When the light returned, Feran was lying on the floor. A hand shook his shoulder. There were voices apparently asking questions, but in some strange tongue. He tried to stand up but his legs gave out and he collapsed.

~

Later, he came to lying flat on his back dressed in what felt like a simple shroud. He shouted and struggled, felt a sharp pain in his arm and then his limbs became very heavy. A huge weight pushed him down, down into blackness.

~

When he woke again everything was calm.

'Do *** hear ***?' This was possibly a question in the

language of the Roman soldiers, but spoken with a strange accent. He couldn't make sense of many of the words. Turning to look at the speaker all he could make out was the usual indistinct shadow.

'What happened to me?'

'I *** *** you. Did you see the man who *** in the chariot?

Feran found he was becoming accustomed to the unusual accent. It was a truly strange chariot.

'I found the chariot with its door open. When I stepped inside out of the rain, the door closed.'

'Was there anyone else near the chariot?'

'No, I didn't see anyone. Where am I?'

'Don't worry about where we are. You're ill and l can make you better. Rest.'

Feran tried to move his left arm but it was trapped. Another sharp pain and falling into blackness.

~

'I've given you herbs to clear your lungs.' The female voice sounded friendly and reassuring. He took a few deep breaths and was surprised to find the usual tightness in his chest was gone. His nose was completely free of congestion. In all, he felt better than he had for years.

'I also understand you have difficulty seeing?'

Feran nodded.

'If you agree to help me, I can cure the problem with your eyes.'

He didn't believe there was any cure for his poor eyesight. In vain he had tried the ministrations of every shaman and healer for miles around, even the Roman medical facilities at the fort. However, the improvement to his chest showed what this woman was capable of.

'Yes, anything to have my good eyesight back.'

~

Feran was wearing his old clothes patched and made unnaturally clean.

'I've completed my part of the bargain and corrected your sight.' The attractive young woman had short blond hair and was dressed in a strange white tunic. Around her eyes she wore an unusual piece of jewellery, two large gold rings balancing on her nose. With an encouraging smile, she held up a piece of stiff paper. 'Here's a painting of a man called Wilbur. In return for your eyesight I ask you to find this man and return him to the chariot. You may be able to persuade him. He knows he has caused us many problems and they can only be corrected if he returns. He must return. Use trickery or even force if necessary.'

Feran examined the painting. It was, in every way, a very detailed likeness. Even held close to the eye, he couldn't make out the brush strokes.

'If you do this, as well as your restored sight, I will give two pounds of silver denarii. You have also been provided with something which will help you find the chariot, even in the dark.' The woman grasped his left hand and turned it palm down. With two fingers she tapped firmly on the back of his hand. He flinched as his hand seemed to catch fire with an eerie green flame, but there was no heat or pain. Turning his hand over he saw the palm glowing bright green.

'The arrowhead always points towards the chariot. Move your hand around and see how it changes.' In the centre of his glowing palm was the outline of an arrowhead. As he moved it rotated, always pointing in the same direction. 'You put out the light by tapping twice on the back of your hand. Only use this when absolutely necessary, it won't last long.' With the green light extinguished he examined the palm of his hand. There was nothing to see which would explain where the light came from.

~

It was daylight when Feran stepped from the chariot. He pressed the palm of his hand on the place he'd been shown to close the door. Standing back, he was amazed at how well the chariot blended into the forest colours. The woman dressed in white hadn't set a time limit for finding Wilbur. However, there had been a suggestion his improved eyesight might not continue if he wasn't successful. Being reminded how much he depended on his eyes meant he would do anything to please her.

Where to start the search? The fort was the closest place a traveller might find shelter, but he wasn't ready for another confrontation with Tolan. The local village was only a little further away.

The weather had improved and he could try to make sense of what had happened as he walked to the settlement. The promise he had made, two pounds of denarii, his renewed health, in the end it was curiosity which proved decisive. He had to find Wilbur and discover more about what was going on.

As he entered the village, Feran hunched over and lent on his staff trying to recreate his previous posture. He didn't want people asking difficult questions. Eyes averted and squinting through half closed eyelids he tried to hide how his sight had improved. Tapping the ground, he shuffled towards the public water fountain. In the past, he had spent many hours sitting close to the fountain where he could find out all the latest gossip. Occasionally, someone would take pity on a blind man and offer a bite to eat.

Usually the talk was of little consequence, but today he could tell by the tone of the chatter there was something important to discuss.

'Did you hear the scandal about Arleigh?'

'The village elder's daughter? The one betrothed to the Centurion?'

'The very same.'

'No, I haven't heard anything. I've been away at my mother-in-law's funeral.'

'Well, two days ago a man broke into the elder's house and tried to make off with her.'

'How terrible. Is she alright?'

'She fought with the attacker as he dragged her into the woods, but I think she's unharmed.'

'Did he get away?'

'No. Fortunately, the dogs ran him down not far from

the village.'

'I'll bet it was a soldier.'

'Possibly, but nobody knows who he is or where he comes from. He's not saying anything.'

'Where is he now?'

'In the fort waiting until the Centurion returns from his patrol up north amongst the barbarians. Then he'll probably get a good flogging if he escapes with his life.'

~

Feran had heard enough. This could be the person he was sent to find, but a kidnapper and molester, was he the person the woman in white was seeking? Surely not.

~

It was late evening. The main gates of the fort were barred, but the wicket gate remained open for foot traffic. The guards had drunk the bribes provided by those who wanted the cover of darkness to move in or out of the fort while avoiding undue scrutiny. With the alcohol and warmth from the braziers, they were obviously having trouble staying awake. Feran slipped inside without challenge. He knew the layout of the buildings and made his way directly to the cells.

'Wilbur.'

With a start, the prisoner pushed himself to a sitting position and searched the surrounding gloom.

'How do you know my name? Nobody knows my real name.'

Without answering, Feran drew back the bolt on the cell door and swung it open.

'My leg's chained.'

'Here, let me see.'

Feran tapped the back of his left hand and used the light to examine the lock, a very familiar design, possibly one he himself had made. He removed the pin holding his cloak and began probing the lock mechanism. There weren't any surprises and after only two attempts Wilbur's leg was free.

'Stay close to me and keep your head down. If you're found trying to escape your punishment probably won't wait until the Centurion returns.'

~

As they made their way through the wicket gate, Tolan stepped from the shadows. 'Feran! You've a nerve coming back here.'

Tolan raised his vine stick and then paused for an instant as though deciding how to inflict the most pain. Feran used this hesitation to step in close so there wasn't room to strike a blow. Pushing forward, he grasped the stick while unbalancing his opponent. As Tolan struggled to remain upright Feran snatched the stick and stepped away. Then, with a swift movement, he broke it across his knee and threw the pieces into the brazier. Tolan was transfixed as though he couldn't believe what had just happened. He offered no resistance as Feran followed Wilbur into the night.

When they were deep in the forest Feran checked the glowing arrowhead to confirm the direction to the chariot.

'You don't understand. I can't leave without my Arleigh.'

'In the village, I heard you attacked her and dragged her into the forest.'

'That was a story we concocted. When it looked as though we'd be captured, I persuaded her to scratch my face and claim I'd forced her to go with me.'

Wilbur came to a stubborn halt and cast about as though trying to work out the direction to the village.

'Arleigh is coming with me and I won't let anyone stand in my way.'

Feran tried to decide the best way of dealing with the situation while completing his side of the bargain with the woman in white.

'If you come and wait beside the chariot, I'll go to the village and bring Arleigh to you.'

~

Feran was well known to the guard dogs and they allowed him to approach the elder's house in exchange for few friendly pats. He risked tapping on the wooden shutters.

'Feran, what're you doing here. You know I could wake the whole household with a single cry?'

'I'm here because of the man who tried to run away with you.'

'What of him?'

'He's escaped from the fort and is hiding in the forest.'

'If you know where he is why don't you tell the soldiers?'

'Tell the soldiers? I thought you loved him.'

Arleigh shook her head vigorously.

'I'm trying to persuade him to go away, but he insists he loves you and won't leave without you.'

'That's completely ridiculous. I have absolutely no interest in him and never have.'

'Perhaps you could tell him face to face? It may be the only way to get rid of him.'

'Will he really leave if I can convince him I want nothing more to do with him?'

'I hope so.'

With amazing agility, she climbed out of the window. Perhaps this wasn't the first time? They hurried into the woods.

~

Wilbur heard them approach and rushed forwards to embrace Arleigh.

'No, don't touch me. You are nothing to me. Leave before I tell the soldiers where you are.'

'But I love you. I remember the way you looked at me when we first met. I have always treasured that moment.'

'You're mistaken. Just go!'

Rather than accepting this rejection he advanced towards Arleigh. Feran stepped between them but was knocked to the ground.

He heard the crunching of bracken under foot and splintering of small branches as Wilbur struggled to catch up with Arleigh. The ground was treacherous with a scattering of slippery boulders partly hidden amongst grassy tussocks and bracken. There was the sound of a heavy fall, a loud snap, followed by a cry of agony.

By the green glow from his hand Feran found Wilbur sprawled amongst the bracken with his left leg twisted at an impossible angle. With difficulty, he dragged the casualty into the chariot. He pressed the red button twice before stepping outside and allowing the door to close.

~

Over time the glow from Feran's hand grew dimmer and there was no longer an arrowhead. However, one day as he used the light to search for a bee's nest in a hollow tree, the arrowhead returned. He didn't want to meet Wilbur again, but was curious to find out if the chariot had returned. The arrow indicated a path through the woods and into a small clearing. There was no chariot to be seen. He was saddened to find the glow had now faded completely no matter how many times he tapped the back of his hand. This had been his final link with the woman in white, or perhaps not quite final. His eyesight was still totally clear. Disappointed he turned to leave and then saw a leather bag hanging from a tree branch. Untying the bag, he lifted it down. It seemed to weigh about two pounds. Now, he had a comfortable sum of money and his newfound health. He was not quite sure what to do next. **But he would think of something.**[11]

---

[11] Last line from *2001: A Space Odyssey*, Arthur C. Clarke

The Governor Goes Skiing 1963

Gordon J R Smith

Wally Deans and I were employed by the State Electricity Commission (SEC) as High Plains Patrolmen on the Kiewa Hydro-Electric Scheme. Together with other members of the High Plains Patrol, we were responsible for the maintenance of the aqueducts, ancillary plant and equipment on the Bogong High Plains in conjunction with the Rocky Valley Dam and Reservoir. The water from this reservoir is fed by tunnel and pipeline to power four hydro-electric power stations on the Scheme.

During the first week of August 1963, Wally, the foreman of the High Plains Patrol, was advised that we were to meet the Governor of Victoria, Sir Rowan Delacombe, at the Falls Creek car park during the week when the weather was fine and sunny. Wally would be notified of the time and day we were to take the Governor in the Sno-Cat for a few hours skiing on the tows in the Falls Creek 'Basin' as it was called in those days.

Sir Rowan Delacombe had only just been appointed Governor of Victoria, and he and his wife were making a tour of North East Victoria. Included in their itinerary was a visit to the State Electricity Commission's Kiewa Hydro-Electric Scheme. His visit to Falls Creek would be quite an honour for us and no doubt a pleasure for him, because he was said to be a good skier.

We were given the dimensions of the Vice Regal flag post, so that I could make up a holder to secure the vice-regal flag to the bonnet of the Sno-Cat. I quickly constructed the flag-holder and attached it to the bonnet of the Sno-Cat, ready for the appointed day. Wally Deans was instructed that he was to drive the Sno-Cat, and I was to go along to assist him as usual.

We didn't have long to wait for Sir Rowan to have his day on the snow, because the following day was fine and sunny. We were notified to proceed to Falls Creek to meet the Governor at 1 pm. I checked everything and gave the Sno-Cat a thorough clean, especially the windows, before we drove down about an hour earlier to get the Sno-Cat in position with the wheels up and the skis downs ready ready to go up the track to the Falls Creek ski area.

Right on the appointed time Sir Rowan arrived in a shiny black Daimler. His chauffeur handed us the vice-regal flag from his car, which I put on the Sno-Cat. Thankfully, it fitted perfectly. Sir Rowan was a most imposing looking gentleman, with thick white hair and white moustache. He was dressed in ski gear and boots.

While Wally was being introduced to Sir Rowan, the driver took the Governor's skis from the boot, which I attached to the rack on top of the Sno-Cat. Wally helped Sir Rowan into the front seat beside him and I climbed into the back seat. With a roar from the large Chrysler straight-eight engine, and with the steel tracks clattering noisily, off we went up to the Basin, We parked in front of the Bogong Ski Club, where I gave Sir Rowan his skis and watched while he put them on. Then with a wave and a thank you, Wally and I stood by the Sno-Cat and watched as Sir Rowan sidestepped up towards the ski tow on the Frying Pan Spur.

The tow operators had been told beforehand of the visit and he was waved straight through to the tow. We wanted to see some vice-regal skiing and we were not disappointed. He rode the tow expertly and it was easy to tell he had ridden on a tow previously. We watched as he skied down in the Arlberg style of linked stem-christie turns. It was obvious that he was no novice. He had most likely skied in various resorts in Europe where he once served as an officer of the British sector in Berlin for three years.

While we were waiting, we had a few questions from skiers, wanting to have a look and ask about the Sno-Cat, and in particular, the small flag flying on the front. Some were quite surprised to find that the Governor of Victoria was a skier and was skiing on the Pan. I said to Wally that I would like to have a couple of runs on the tow next to where Sir Rowan was skiing. Wally offered no objection to my request, so I had two quick runs on perfect snow before returning to the Sno-Cat. Some two hours later Sir Rowan returned to us saying that he had enjoyed his skiing very much.

After some small talk Wally helped him into the front seat and we drove back down to the car park where the vice-regal flag was transferred back to his Daimler. His skis were put in the boot and with a thank you and a shake of our hands, he was off down to Bogong Lodge, the SEC's VIP residence in Bogong, to enjoy the rest of the day with his wife and his hosts, Wally and Emmy Baldwin.

The next day was another beautiful sunny day. We received word that we were to be prepared to take Sir Rowan's wife, Lady Delacombe, on a trip around the Bogong High Plains. It was suggested that this time we use the Snow Trac. This over snow vehicle was equipped with rubber tracks and the driver sat in the front, separated from the small passenger cabin at the back.

Just after noon we were asked to take the Snow Trac down to Falls Creek to pick up Lady Delacombe's party. Rod McDowell, a competent driver of the Snow Trac, drove Wally and me down to the Falls Creek car park. Unlike the Sno-Cat, the Snow Trac was able to be driven straight off the snow and onto the bitumen of the car park, where we waited for Lady Delacombe's party to arrive.

We only had a short time to wait before an SEC utility arrived with Greg Stuart at the wheel. Greg was the engineer in charge of most of the operations above Bogong, which included the High Plains Patrol. I knew Greg well, as we both lived in Bogong Village. Very soon the Daimler, this time without the vice-regal flag, pulled up alongside us in the car park. Lady Delacombe alighted from the car followed by a big black dog, which she referred to as Zara. The chauffeur introduced us to Lady Delacombe, while Greg introduced Rod, Wally and me.

We helped Lady Delacombe, an elegant middle-age woman dressed for the journey in sensible clothes, into the back seat of the Snow Trac. Her big black setter dog, Zara, climbed in after her and lay on the floor at her feet. Greg, Wally and I climbed aboard beside her. Rod had been told to drive up to Rocky Valley, cross the dam wall and head for Langford's Gap, so off we went around Windy Corner.

It was a wise choice to use Snow Trac; with its rubber tracks and small Porsche engine, it was much quieter than the Sno-Cat and provided a far more comfortable ride. As we trundled along there was hardly a word spoken. Greg was not pointing out any of the landmarks we passed, not even as we crossed the dam wall. I don't think anyone knew what to say, until Lady Delacombe 'broke the ice' mentioning that she loved the snow country of Switzerland and Austria, but this snow-covered country was totally different to anything she had seen before.

I decided at this point that I would keep the conversation going. I told Lady Delacombe that I agreed with her, as I had travelled through Europe and skied in

Switzerland and Austria. So, while Greg and Wally remained mute, I talked quite naturally with Lady Delacombe, pointing out to her various features of the snow-covered Bogong High Plains during the journey out to Langford's Gap and back. Zara, the dog, didn't join in the conversation, nor did she move a muscle for the entire journey.

When we arrived back at the car park, Lady Delacombe thanked us all for taking her on such a lovely trip, then turning to me, she said she had enjoyed talking to me about Europe.

At the close of Sir Rowan and Lady Delacombe's official visit to the Kiewa Scheme, they were to be farewelled by the school children from the one-teacher Bogong Primary School. The children were sent home at lunchtime to clean-up and change into any scouting or other uniforms they had. From kindergarten and up, there were nineteen students in all. They planned to line the road at the intersection of the Upper Kiewa Valley Road, and the road down to the school, to wave farewell to the Governor's car as it passed by. The new teacher, Bob Richardson, rang my wife Dilys when the time was approaching, to ask her if she would come down to the school to help him get all the children up to the corner to meet the Governor. Dilys straight away went down to the school to help.

The farewell to the Governor and his wife by the school children is best told in this poem Dilys wrote shortly after the visit.

Bogong School's Farewell
Nineteen children hurried home
And quickly ate their lunch,
Cleaned and tidied up themselves,
With vim and lots of punch.

Back along the road to school
To where the ground was shady;
They played until the time came
To meet the Governor and his Lady.

In ones and twos they climbed the track,
Each quietly as a mouse,
Till nearly at the corner
Some at the corner house

A patrolman called out 'Hurry'
And the children promptly ran
Arriving at the corner,
Saw a lady and a man.

But, more surprises were in store;
For, who else should they be?
But those very eminent people
They'd come uphill to see!

The Governor shook hands with a few,
The cubs, the scouts, the guides,
Their teacher (lady helper shook hands too)
And a few other folks besides.

The Governor declared a holiday,
'Thank you' the children said,
A few more laughs and back to the car
Waiting for them up ahead.

The children ran across from the car.
Waving their flags on the way.
The Governor called out 'One big shout'
And the children shouted 'Hooray'

The car moved off, slowly at first
And more hoorays shook the air,
Sending them off with a happy sound
While the children continued to stare

For its not every Governor who leaves his car
When his tight schedule is right up to date,
And smilingly stands on a cold windy road
To greet nineteen children running late!

Dilys Terry Smith

I am sure the Governor and his wife left the Kiewa Hydro-Electric Scheme with an appreciation of the beauty and variety of the high country of this part of the Victorian Alps. As for myself, during the ten years I worked on the Kiewa Scheme, I was employed on many diverse and exciting worksites, pumping concrete, tunnel boring, rock crushing, to name a few. None so unique however, as the two days we took the Governor and his wife to visit the snows of the Bogong High Plains, and for all of these experiences **I have been grateful for every minute of it.** [12]

---

[12] Last line from *The Museum of Words*, Georgia Blain

Reflections

Erica Tippett

The old man raised the tarnished mirror with a shaking hand and looked in. He waited, blinking his eyes slowly. There was no reflection, only a dull cloudy grey. He lowered the antique and placed it carefully on the table beside him, thinking of the day the King had awarded him the mirror as a parting gift for his many years of service. Turning his head to the window, the overcast world that lay beyond his little shack was quiet, still, unenticing. He shuffled back down on his bed and closed his heavy eyes. Sleep came easily.

When the old man awoke the sun was low in the sky, shining through the window. He looked out and spied the girl, walking up the road. She carried a newspaper under her arm and skipped up the stone steps two at a time. The old man smiled, ambled over to his armchair and sat down. The girl knocked on the door. 'Come in.'

'Uncle, I have brought you the day's news.'

'Thank you. You are a good girl. Here, give it to me.'

The girl handed him the paper and perched on the small stool. The old man scanned the front page and opened the paper. The girl looked at him intently, bouncing her left knee. He turned the pages with purpose. 'Did you go see the lions again?' the girl asked, eyes wide.

The old man lowered the paper and looked into the girl's green-blue eyes. 'Yes,' he said. 'They were magnificent.'

'Will you take me next time? Please?'

'My darling girl, your parents wouldn't like that now, would they?' the old man said.

The girl looked down at her feet. 'No. I know. But it's not fair. I want to see the lions.' Tears welled in the girl's eyes.

'And you would love them,' the old man said with a sigh, looking out the window. 'But your parents think I am irresponsible.'

The girl sprang up from the stool and grabbed the old man's arm. 'But they are wrong! It's not your fault I got lost that day. Please Uncle, take me to see the lions! Just one time and I will never ask again, I promise.'

The old man thought for a moment, then nodded. 'Okay,' he said, 'I can take you one time to see the lions. But you must promise not to tell your parents.'

'Oh, thank you Uncle. Yes, I promise!'

~

'Are you ready?' the old man asked the girl.

'Yes, Uncle,' she replied, biting the side of her lip.

'And you packed your backpack just as I told you?'

'Yes, I have everything you asked for. Except the apples. I could only get two. I heard mama coming down the hall and couldn't risk her seeing me.'

'Two apples. It's not ideal but hopefully it's enough to stave off the sickness. Now take my hand and whatever you do, don't let go.' The old man raised the mirror. His reflection was crystal clear. He pictured the lions in his mind's eye and stared into the mirror. The plains of Africa came into view and there they were, lying in the grass, three beautiful lions.

'Mirror of Eurynome,

let us be where we can see,

let me bring my friend with me,

take us to the lions,' the old man boomed, gripping the mirror and the girl's delicate hand.

The world spun, colours shone, and the pair were gone from the little shack by the sea. They landed in the long grass face down, still holding hands. The old man rolled over and swiftly sat up, blinking the world into view. 'We are here child, help me up.'

The girl didn't move. The old man grabbed the backpack on her back and heaved as hard as he could. The backpack rose a little, but the girl didn't. The old man scrambled to his feet and spun around. Sweat beaded on his brow. 'We are here Laila; come and see the lions,' he said leaning over the girl. 'Oh, dear, you have the travel sickness.'

He shuffled the backpack off the girl's back and rested it on the ground. The sun beat down from a cloudless sky. He found the water canister and splashed water on the girl's face. She stirred and sat up. 'How are you feeling darling girl?'

'Dizzy,' the girl said, raising a hand to her pale forehead.

'It'll pass soon, here bite into this.' The old man offered an apple. The girl ate some and her colour returned to normal.

'Take a look through the binoculars,' the old man said, putting the strap over the girl's head.

'I see them!' she exclaimed. 'Can we go a little closer?'

'Yes, a little. But we must be careful, we don't know where the male is. He won't be far off and will likely be back soon.' They crept closer, staying low to the ground. When the old man looked through the binoculars again, he put out his hand instinctively as if he could touch the lions. 'Magnificent,' he whispered.

The girl beamed. The two sat in silence and watched the big cats lazing in the sun. The biggest of the females yawned showing her sharp teeth. 'Wow,' the girl gasped.

~

The sun was getting low when the old man awoke. He sat up and saw the backpack, but no girl. He looked around but could only see grass, plains and the purpling sky. He struggled to his feet and shuffled to the bag. His hand touched the cold metal of the mirror. The old man pulled it out and peered in. There was no reflection, only the dull grey of inactivity. 'Don't panic,' he murmured, returning the mirror to the bag. He grabbed the remaining apple and swung the bag onto his back. He took a large bite and chewed, peering in all directions. He saw a flash of colour in his peripheral vision. The old man turned to see three men wearing khaki uniforms and black and red bandannas push the child into a waiting Jeep. 'Hey, stop!' he yelled and hobbled towards the car. 'Laila! No!' The doors slammed and the idle became a roar as the vehicle surged forward. The old man reached the road just in time to see the car turn left at the fork. The dust made him cough as he hurried along the road to the village.

~

Darkness lay heavy across the rapidly-cooling earth by the time the old man saw the lights of the village. He hesitated at the junction, kicking a stone with his dusty boot and murmuring to himself. 'Right to schoolteacher, left to nurse.' He took the water from the backpack and drank a small sip, pursing his lips together. He trudged on, slower than before. The teacher's hut lay dark at the front of the rudimentary school. The old man went inside. All was silent. He rested his head on the backpack like a pillow and went to sleep.

~

'Hello?' a voice murmured. The old man felt a warm hand gently shaking him. He blinked his eyes open to the dim light of a candle and the concerned face of the teacher.

'Hello, friend,' the old man said. The teacher leant over and gave the man a warm embrace. Her smile changed to a frown.

'You must go. Not safe here,' she whispered.

'Why? It must be late now. Where can I go in the middle of the night?' the old man asked, rubbing his eyes with the backs of his hands.

The teacher reached out her hand to help him up. 'Bad man come. He not like stranger. He find you, I get big trouble.'

'Bad man? Does he wear a black and red bandanna? I think he took the girl. I brought a girl with me, to see the lions.'

'I saw girl,' the teacher gasped. 'In bad man car. Fast on road. Big trouble. Why bring girl? Not safe.'

'Do you know where they would have taken her? I must find her and take her home.'

'No go to bad man. You old. He bad, bad man. He take girl to market.'

'What market? What do you mean? Oh, they will sell the girl at market!'

'Yes. Go market when sun high,' the teacher said raising her hand straight up overhead.

'What about the nurse? Do you think she will help me?' the old man asked, lifting the backpack to his back.

The teacher nodded. 'Yes, go to nurse. Her husband strong. Go!'

The old man shuffled out of the hut blinking his eyes in search of light in the velvet-black night. The cool midnight air raised bumps on his arms and legs as he stumbled along the road. Every noise was amplified, and with each small step he willed his tired body forward. As he rounded a bend in the road he heard someone coming towards him. The old man froze.

'Dumêla rra,' the stranger said quietly.

'Dumêla, friend,' the old man whispered.

The stranger grabbed the old man's shoulder, pulling him close. 'There are no friends here anymore,' the stranger spat. 'Go! And stay off the road. The night patrol will be back soon.'

The old man kept as best he could to the bushes at the side of the road. Twice he heard the rumble of an engine and had to hide. He lay out of sight, heart thumping in his chest until he was certain the vehicle had gone. In the early morning light, he pulled the mirror out of the dusty bag and turned it over. 'Come on mirror, I need you today. I need your reflection back.' The old man's peering eyes were met with a dreary grey.

~

The old man opened the front door of the medical clinic softly and walked in. The smell of ammonia burned at his throat. He saw the nurse kneeling on the floor, picking up pieces of a broken machine. 'Hello, friend,' the old man said.

The nurse looked up in fright. She had a cut under her right eye and blood stained her white pinafore. The old man reached out a trembling hand to help her up. 'Thank goodness they didn't find you here!' she said, rising to her feet.

'I'm sorry for the trouble,' the old man said.

'Me too.' The nurse sighed.

The old man righted some wooden chairs that lay scattered across the clinic. 'I brought a girl,' he confessed.

'I know about your girl.'

'Will you help me get her back? I went to the teacher's house last night, but she was too afraid.'

'I don't blame her. She has enough girls of her own to worry about. It is a most troubled time. You shouldn't have come. And not with a girl,' the nurse chided. She paused. 'But my family will help you.'

'Oh, thank you, thank you. I didn't dream that things could have become like this. The girl was, well, she wanted to see the lions. I fell asleep, from the travel sickness, you know.'

'You cannot keep travelling like this. Your old body cannot recover like it used to.' She looked him over. 'You look unwell. I will fetch you some medicine,' she said, her tone softening.

~

The marketplace was full of people when the old man arrived with the nurse's husband, nephew and cousin. The big burly men dwarfed the old man. The summer sun had nearly reached its highest point and the heat was oppressive amongst all the bodies. They made their way to a large rusted shed beyond the market stalls. The nephew exchanged a couple of words with the khaki-clad doormen and the group was ushered into the dark. The old man blinked. The shed was filled with men. The rows of buyers stood eagerly, shuffling their sandaled feet and spreading dust into the air. The sellers wore black and red bandannas. A back door opened, the midday sun flooded in along with a line of girls, tied together by rope. The old man gasped when he saw Laila, her sweet face dirty and lined with tear tracks. The rope pulled on her arms as the girl in front was shoved by one of the men. The old man saw the red marks on her body and bit his lip hard.

The bad man stood on an upturned crate and banged the stub of his rifle onto the wood. The room fell silent. He spoke in the local tongue, which even after all these years, the old man had been unable to master. One by one the girls were auctioned to the highest bidder. Bundles of money were counted by three strong men who stood below their leader. Laila was second-last in line. The old man and his crew edged closer to the front, squeezing between the sweaty crowd. The fourth-last girl was taller than all the others, with big eyes and a womanly body. The bidding became frantic. The declared highest bidder handed over his money and one of the men counted it. He shouted to the bidder and shoved some notes back in his face. The purchaser retaliated. The gang member slapped him with the back of his hand and pushed him violently. The crowd parted and let him fall to the dust. The trio began hitting and kicking the man towards the door, yelling and berating him. The man scrambled to get to his feet, but they kept attacking him until he stopped moving, bloodied and beaten, less than a metre from the door.

The auction continued and soon it was Laila's turn.

The nephew bid first, then the cousin, then some other bidders joined in and the bidding got higher and higher until the nephew shook his head. The old man turned to the nurse's husband. 'We have to do something,' he pleaded.

The husband moved closer. 'What can we do, we've been outbid. Even with everyone's contribution we don't have nearly enough.'

'But I can't lose her. What will they do to her? I could never face her parents.' The old man pushed forward through the crowd. 'Laila,' he yelled. She looked up for the first time and her eyes met the old man's. The men stepped in front of the girl. The bidding stopped. 'Please, there's been a mistake,' the old man said, 'this girl belongs to me.'

Rage burned in the bad man's eyes. 'No!' he shouted. 'No mistake. My girl! You pay.'

'But, I …' the old man stammered.

'Stranger; go home! You not welcome!' the bad man signalled to his trio. They stepped forward and grabbed the old man. The husband, nephew and cousin stepped up to the men. The nephew said something the old man couldn't understand.

'You have something, stranger?' the bad man barked. 'Better than money? You give me for girl.'

'No, I can't. It's our … only way home …'

'Show him the mirror,' the cousin insisted. The old man looked at the girl. Tears streamed down her face, dropping like rain into the dust at her bare feet.

'Mirror?' the bad man stepped down from the crate and grabbed the girl. Laila shrieked.

The old man's eyes were filled with fear. 'I have a mirror. It can take you anywhere you want to go. It can take you to … the greatest treasure in the world.'

'What greatest treasure?'

'Let me show you.'

The old man removed his backpack. The trio bristled but their leader raised his hand. The old man pulled out the mirror and turned it over. His reflection came into view and he sighed. He pictured the king's guarded treasure in his mind's eye. The bad man stepped closer and peered in. His mouth fell open. He grabbed at the mirror with both hands and pulled it closer. The old man hung on tight to the handle.

'I swap girl for this gold,' the bad man said.

'Only the mirror can take you there,' the old man said with a gulp.

'Yes, take me. And men,' the bad man gestured to his trio.

'Its magic will not be strong enough for five.'

The bad man looked up from the mirror. 'You not come. We four, get gold. Don't need old man,' the bad man jeered.

The men closed in eagerly on the old man. He looked despairingly at the ancient mirror and passed it toward the bad man, who snatched it. 'You must link hands. And don't let go,' the old man warned. The men linked hands in a circle with the mirror.

'Mirror of Eurynome,' the old man boomed.

'Take them where I can see,

take the four, but leave me,

take them to the treasure.'

Colours swirled and the four were gone. A cloud of dust rose up. The old man fought through it and rushed to Laila, wrapping her in a tight hug. She buried her head in his chest.

~

'Eat, child,' the teacher said kindly. Laila gulped down the broth.

The old man chuckled. 'Easy child, don't give yourself a stomach-ache,' he said. There were footsteps outside the hut.

'Hello?' the nurse called. She entered the hut with her husband close behind. The nephew and cousin came in with their wives and children until the hut was bursting with bodies. 'Good news my friend!' the nurse said when she saw the old man.

'What good news?'

'The villagers are so happy with you for getting rid of the bad man that they have come up with a plan to get you and that dear girl home.' She smiled a broad toothy smile.

'Have they? And what plan is that?'

'Well, you know the farmer whose daughter was last in line? He knows some folk from two villages over who've been doing business with this Italian and he knows a sea captain. They've managed to get you passage on the ship. It's taking goods from the North through the Greek Isles and will be able to drop you off at your port along the way.'

'And I can get you on a truck that's headed to the port tomorrow,' said the cousin beaming.

'That is good news!' the old man said. 'Laila, we're going home!' The girl looked across the table at the old man. She jumped up and hugged the nurse, tears running down her cheeks.

~

The girl clung tightly to the old man's arm, eyes wide in the darkness. She could just make out the rise and fall of the frail frame beside her. Occasionally she heard his heavy breathing above the creaking sounds of the boat. She forced her eyes closed and eventually drifted off into a dreamless sleep. The old man lay on his back, still. His lips curled upwards in a faint smile. **The old man was dreaming of the lions.**[13]

---

[13] Last line from *The Old Man and the Sea*, Ernest Hemingway

Out of Control

By Karen Wescombe

When at home, Mary loved leaving the curtains open so she could see the world around her. It was mid-autumn, and glancing out she observed that darkness would soon envelop her garden. With the windows uncluttered, the connection with her neighbours, her life and the world, seemed stronger.

As she laid the table for dinner, her excitement about the coming evening grew. She gently placed three plates down, one for Bill and one each for the children. She especially chose Lauren's favourite plate, the old-world-pattern dish from England that they'd picked up when they visited Ballarat on holiday, and it was imperative for Mark to have his favourite Spiderman glass.

Mary would not be home tonight. She regretted missing any evening with her family, confident though that they wouldn't miss her with their Dad around. Mary planned to leave everything ready to serve. After tea, they would play a game or two; knowing that cleaning was *not* a top priority, she planned on washing the dishes tomorrow. With a last check that everything was perfect, she gathered her bag. Luckily tonight Bill was the designated parent to pick up Mark from basketball and Lauren from music class.

Sue, her best friend at work, organised a 'ladies catch up' with the other departments, stating it would improve their careers. Men seemed to always be 'networking' and look where it got them. One girl laughed, 'Yeah, off to the golf course twice a week!'. It seemed a good idea when she first agreed. A few hours catching up at the local hotel with friends, having a meal and a relaxing drink, while Bill cared for the kids. It all seemed harmless. Even working for the same company, she never spent enough time with Sue.

'I'm in,' she declared, and they made plans to start the next week. Soon it became a regular weekly activity— WEDNESDAY NIGHT – WORK CATCHUP— marked on work wall calendars and put into diaries. And they enjoyed themselves. It improved their understanding of the business while enhancing their team spirit by encouraging them to support each other in their work areas.

The initial month, they met and chatted before and after eating, yet with so much to say they ended up talking all throughout the meal. Over the following months, other women noticed the positive effects of the dinners and wanted to join. 'No problem,' said Sue with a smile, 'the more the merrier. We may all end up in senior positions working with a golf bag in hand.' And it worked out perfectly, until one night when Jenny joined them for the first time.

Jenny worked in the logistics department. Though Mary never worked with her directly, she noticed others considered her a friendly and helpful colleague. She livened up the conversation relating work transport disasters with a great sense of humour.

As everyone prepared to leave, Jenny announced that, with her husband away travelling, she would stay a short time to wind down. After such an entertaining night, Mary and Stephanie, one of the newer staff members in the accounting area, didn't want the evening to end either, so they announced they'd keep her company. They moved into the lounge area and continued an earlier conversation. After twenty minutes, Stephanie announced her bed was calling her. She wanted to get some beauty sleep as some complicated figures needed completing the next day and she didn't want to be 'off her game'.

After Stephanie left, Jenny spoke to Mary. 'Come on, let's have a flutter for fun; see who can make $5.00 last the longest.'

'Count me in,' Mary answered, happy to enjoy the fun a little longer.

They moved into the gaming area of the hotel and found two machines, side by side, and played small—ten cents a time. After only ten minutes, Mary won a Mini

Jackpot. Ok, it wasn't anything to write home about she mused to herself, $28.66; but the win made the night much more exciting. She now had $31.10 in her purse. Surely that new girl from the accounts department would have approved how she increased her money threefold.

Mary now looked upon Wednesday nights with more anticipation and she organised everything with more spring in her step. She enjoyed the people, loved catching up with all the gossip and news, and when Jenny mentioned staying a little later, she eagerly agreed. They again played modestly and suddenly, in amazement, she won $507 on a feature. While Jenny expressed happiness for her, she left soon after saying, 'I want to be ready, my husband is due home'. Mary nodded, leaving at the same time as Jenny, planning how she would spend her winnings.

The next date Jenny didn't turn up, a conference required her presence and her apologies were sent. A little down over the meal—it'd been a little quieter—Mary acknowledged to herself that she had been looking forward to her time with Jenny. When the others started to leave, Mary announced she'd pop into the bathroom. They expressed their goodbyes and Mary let them leave. She'd had fun with Jenny and she reasoned she could easily amuse herself while enjoying some quiet time alone. She'd brought $100, that should be enough if luck ran her way. Unfortunately, luck did not run with her. She loathed going home without her original stake, so she withdrew $100 from the ATM and slid it into the mouth of the machine to win her stake back. Tonight though, the plan to win failed and the machine just ate her money giving her nothing back.

She walked out to the bus considering the change in her luck, decided that her run was over, and now was a good time to bow out gracefully. She also experienced a wave of shame at her fascination with the poker machines. When Wednesday night came around again, she still took $100 from her winnings and popped it into her purse 'just in case'. If Jenny turned up it would be rude not to stay, she enjoyed their chats. Jenny wasn't there though—her kids needed picking up from a school event. Mary tried to stay focused and enjoy all the chatter, yet she impatiently waited for the meal to be over, thinking of some 'me' time. *This time will be different'. 'I've done it before—I can do it again'*, she thought.

She moved to the gaming lounge and settled on her 'lucky' machine, the one she had previously won the feature on. Every other machine though seemed to beckon her to *choose me, choose me.* At first, it seemed that she may have a good night, the lights flashed so much she laughed *I'll have to put my sunglasses on if this continues!* She upped her bet—first to fifty cents, moving next to a dollar a spin. 'They pay out more when you bet larger,' declared the man next to her. 'Yes, that would make sense,' she agreed. 'The higher I bet, the more the things will respond.'

She moved her bet up to two dollars a spin and then increased it to three. She didn't seem to realise that the other player lost all his money after betting high, moving off his machine fifteen minutes later. A big cheer arose behind her and she looked to see that someone had won $210. *Must be new, a regular would not be happy with that*, she decided. She pressed and pressed, mesmerised by the symbols, willing them to form a pattern that could, should, would, show that she was clever, lucky, successful. The lights flashed: the music played … yet her money dwindled. The extra symbols needed to make the feature start, or get that elusive five in a row, were conspicuously absent. And then the machine buzzed, wouldn't spin, and she realised that her money had evaporated. A little saddened, she caught the bus just before it moved on. 'Time passes quickly when you're playing. I must set the alarm on the phone so that doesn't happen again', she mumbled to herself as she climbed aboard.

The week dragged. She had trouble concentrating on work matters or things at home. She'd hardly said anything to Sue in days. Several times Bill or the kids had to repeat something, or nudge her. 'So who's in dreamland now?' She looked forward to Wednesday, though a slight nagging had formed in her mind (which she ignored), as she glamorised the fun Wednesday nights brought to her. No wins recently, however she just *knew* that she would be a winner this week.

The next week, rushing to the bus she realised she was twenty minutes too early. 'It must be an omen,' she said to herself, *tonight will be the night!*

The meal was lovely and two new women joining the group enthralled everyone with their stories, yet her own mind appeared to be elsewhere. She ached to make her fortune and fairly pushed her friends into their cars.

Are you sure you don't want a lift, Mary? asked Kate, 'I go right past your door'.

'No, no, Bill will pick me up with the kids,' she lied. It was the first of many lies she was to acknowledge making.

She nearly tripped over rushing to 'her' machine when another person aimed for it. The thought came unbidden to her mind, *this is my machine, how dare they,* as she sat down. She barely registered the other players. Some regulars, some newbies, those with hope in their eyes, those with down-turned mouths. She heard patrons repeating 'please, please, please' to their machines, as she would do many times herself in the coming months. She put in fifty dollars, quickly pressed and waited for a lucky spin. Fiddlesticks! Nothing! *Oh well, this time,* pressing the button. It must happen this time! However, yet again, nothing happened, her money was gone. *Maybe I should move to another machine? No, it must pay out soon, one more note.* She slipped another fifty into the note acceptor, her excitement renewed until that note also disappeared— disappearing even quicker than the first one had.

She placed a RESERVED sign on her machine and went to the bathroom. The internal dialogue kept up— *What should I do? Try again? Going home would be sensible. Surely, I'll win this time.* She withdrew one hundred dollars, embarrassed having to ask a staff member to provide her with her own money. She justified the withdrawal by reasoning that she would replace it with her winnings. Her heartbeat raced and then a wave of anger spread through her. Nothing. No feature! Nothing! She saw out of the corner of her eye another player muttering to themselves. 'They're right, the machines are not behaving themselves tonight,' she mused. Her phone alarm went off reminding her of the bus arrival and she reset it for another hour, it must pay off any moment and I can catch the next bus, she reflected.

Another hundred withdrawn—oh, well, back to where I started so not a total disaster. 'In for a penny, in for a pound,' she said, remembering the quote that her parents used to repeat.

Pressing the buttons, the machine noise persisted relentlessly, yet for all the lights and noise, the money disappeared bit by bit. Down to her last twenty, the machine would give her some credits to keep going and then the cycle would repeat itself, up and down. A headache developed yet stopping wasn't an option. People came and sat at the surrounding machines, some tried to start up conversations, yet she couldn't talk, her focus was on the machine and she was there to win, not talk. Her money now gone; she ran for the late bus. Scrambling for her ticket, pleased she had a daily ticket to make it home.

Mary felt confused and frustrated. *What is wrong with me? I've never been out of control before—never! I'm always the sensible one, the one everyone relies on for advice and help when they have problems.*

She started slipping away from work, a longer lunch here, a little late for work another day, losing herself in the bright lights and repetitive electronic jingles. Things didn't improve as she hoped and she found herself lost in a cocoon world, one getting tighter and tighter as the weeks passed. Different days, different times, different venues. She glimpsed tradies in high visibility vests, the elderly, and businessmen. The elderly she understood. A place to keep warm or cool. But the businessmen, well, they wouldn't be here if they weren't winning, she reflected. Upon entering the venues, she felt the control of the gaming machines. The ringing bells, flashing lights and electronic music possessed her again. She knew that she shouldn't be there, yet she also knew she couldn't leave. She had to make good; her last chance to fix everything. 'I can't stop now, the feature may be next and then all will be well,' she would say to herself to justify being there.

For three months she longed only to play the machines. The last months had been disastrous, she acknowledged. However, she knew it was possible to win, hadn't she'd done it before? The rational side of her realised that she had quite a few losses to catch up on before becoming a 'winner' again, however that Jackpot still stood ready and waiting for her. She could not stop, and the only issue became where to get some stake money—then she remembered the holiday money hidden in the bottom drawer of the dresser.

That night it was like she was in a war zone, waging a losing battle with unbeatable machines. Her money went up; her money went down. A couple of times she thought of cashing out, yet her balance didn't cover her losses and she feared moving may result in 'annoying' the machine.

Finally, at 2.30am she stumbled out of the door. She was unbalanced, not from drinking, but from exhaustion and distress. Too devastated and depressed to even smile at security, she slipped out the front doors and headed to the bus stop. She sat down on the bench, there were no people around. *Why would there be at this time of the morning?* The tears flowed, the sobbing unrelenting. It appeared she had sunk into quicksand with no way out, unable to breathe, drowning. She felt a burning self-hatred, deeper than any emotion she had experienced before as she fully comprehended her position—she had lost everything.

Time passed and then it started to rain, yet she still did not move. Where could she go? The buses had finished; phoning home wasn't an option. Five kilometres, not far in a vehicle yet in the middle of the night, in the rain, walking? Nothing more than what she deserved, she reflected. Luckily, she could cry with no shame as the rain covered the tear tracks. How could she have behaved so stupidly? She'd walked a couple of kilometres before she stumbled on piles of gumnuts dropped by trees in the wind. As she straightened up, a car stopped, and the driver got out. Great, now someone plans on robbing me—no-one's fault but my own, it's what I deserve.

'Hello. May I offer you a lift?' She noticed it was one of the staff members from the hotel kitchen. She remembered his politeness and smile when he had delivered their meals.

'No, I just fell. I'm ok, I haven't far to go,' Mary replied, not wanting him to see her in this condition.

'Now, I won't take "no" for an answer. It would upset my mum terribly if I didn't help a regular customer, especially someone who always piled up the used dishes to help,' he said with a smile.

Mary returned his smile, probably the first one for the evening. Maybe even the week she confessed to herself.

'That's very kind of you. I'm just down on Wilmott Street.'

'Well, hop in before you drown. I'm Peter, by the way.'

The car had not warmed up fully; however, it was a welcome reprieve from outside.

'I, I missed the last bus,' Mary explained.

'My mum told me always to keep my nose out of other people's business; however, she also said that when folks need help, be there for them'.

Mary sneezed.

'You don't seem as happy as when you first used to come in for dinner with your group. I wish whatever is making you so sad would stop.'

'Now,' he brightly commented a few minutes later, 'we nearly have you home, where would you like me to drop you'.'

She looked over at this young man and wondered how he got to be so perceptive, he must have some special mum.

'Just here thanks, number fifteen,' whispered Mary.

As she got out of the car, she knew she had been given another chance; someone had broken the spell.

'Thank You, Peter, for the ride and your help.'

As she walked to the front door, she realised that money wasn't the real reason she had gambled; it was more to escape, to feel as though she was in control, to test herself. It had been an illusion, and now she knew what she had to do. As she tiptoed into the house, she looked at all she could have lost and knew that she'd never slip that low again. It wasn't the end. **It was a beginning**.[14]

---

[14] Last Line from *Hark*, Ed McBain

About the Authors

Mube Akinci-Desem

Mube's passion for writing is a life-long affair; she used to write little short stories and 1-2 verse poems during primary school. Her articles, short stories and poems have been published in newspapers and anthologies and she is in the process of having her first book published.

Mube likes to read historical and science fiction novels. Her love of travelling and thirst for different cultures has taken her around the world to some of the most unexpected places in Europe and Asia. Mube also loves to sit and enjoy cups of coffee with friends in cosmopolitan coffee shops around Melbourne. Mube enjoys walking, sometimes her long walks may extend as far as the CBD.

Sasha Buntman

Sasha Buntman is passionate about communicating, organising, digital marketing and independent publishing.

Her purpose in life has always revolved around the art of organising. Organising the layout of elements on your page or in your book; organising words, sentences and messages together to create something meaningful and worthwhile for your audience.

As the founder of Midnight Media, Sasha provides affordable self-publishing solutions for fiction and non-fiction. Sasha project manages everything for you and ensures that your self-publishing journey runs smoothly and successfully.

Copywriting is another obsession of Sasha's. Her subsidiary business, Midnight Marketing, provides digital marketing support services to authors and entrepreneurs: including email, website and social media content management; copywriting; advertising and more.

Ingrid Fry

Ingrid is the author of the soon to be published Crystal Sphere series—a set of speculative fiction thrillers set in Australia—and two self-illustrated children's books. An astrologer who prepared her chart many years ago said, 'your destiny is to be either a nun, or a writer'. For Ingrid, the choice was a no-brainer, even though writing sometimes makes her feel as cloistered as a nun.

A writer, business development consultant, and minder of a husband and a beagle with super-powers, she lives in a leafy suburb on the outskirts of Melbourne. When she's not writing, you can find her pistol shooting at the local gun club, dancing her socks off at The

Caravan Music Club, or being a passionate karateka, inching ever closer to a black belt in karate.

Sakuntala Gananathan

Sakuntala is a retired chartered accountant. Her historical novel *White Flowers of Yesterday* was published in the US and was awarded Editor's Choice by her publishers, iUniverse.

An excerpt of their appraisal: 'The author has done a fantastic job of weaving setting, characterisation, historical information, dialogue and plot together to create a complete, unique and compelling story...' while *Kirkus Review* wrote '...a surfeit of grace and wit...'

Sakuntala takes an active interest in the Tamil Senior Citizens Fellowship (Victoria) Inc, a non-profit association, of which she is the honorary treasurer for the current year. In 2013 her short story, 'Mend a Bend', earned her a prize at the Monash Word Fest Short Story Competition.

Ruth Kweitel

Ruth Kweitel left school after completing year 11, to study nursing at the Royal Melbourne Hospital. After working for 13 years as a general nurse, she went to Royal Park Psychiatric Hospital to study psychiatric nursing. She spent the remainder of her career working in mental health. Ruth began tertiary education as a mature-age student. She completed a Bachelor of Arts (Psychology / Sociology), Graduate Diploma in Applied Psychology and Doctor of Philosophy and obtained registration as a psychologist. Her shift work employment enabled Ruth to undertake her tertiary studies while working full time. She intended to write a textbook on completion of her PhD but was too exhausted to do it. After retirement, Ruth began to dabble in writing fiction and has now made that a part of her retirement activities.

Marlene Laurent

Born in Australia Marlene grew up in the post-war suburb of South Oakleigh. Brought up a Catholic, she entered the convent at the age of 17 after attending boarding school in Fremantle, WA. She left the convent following the Ecumenical Council when changes were implemented in the Catholic Church.

She worked in an office in South Melbourne for a short time where she met her husband Jim. Soon after she went to Toorak Teacher's college and completed a teaching degree. Later she studied to add to her qualifications completing a Bachelor of Teaching and an ED Admin certificate. She taught at Brighton Primary before having her daughter Monica, and at Noble Park Primary on her return from family leave.

Teaching became a passion. She was actively involved in education in the Victorian system and, during her career, implemented many changes to the curriculum at her schools. She became an Assistant Principal at Brandon Park Primary and then Principal at Oakwood Park Primary and finally at Glenferrie Primary. She played basketball and tennis and attended the gym regularly to keep fit.

On retiring she decided to have a go at writing, something she had always enjoyed doing. She is a member of the Caulfield Writer's Group and the Monash Writer's group. This short story is her third attempt to get her work published.

Marlene Lives in East Bentleigh and spends her time cycling, keeping fit at the local gym, reading, writing and travelling. She is member of the Australian Conservation Association, The Wilderness Society and other conservation groups. She takes an interest in her local community, as Secretary of the Glen Eira Residents Association.

Sung-Ju Suya Lee

Suya received a BFA from York University, Canada, an MBA from Bradford University School of Management, UK, and a PhD in Media & Communication from RMIT University, Australia. As part of her creative practice PhD, she wrote a farce comedy screenplay, which was long-listed for the ScreenCraft Comedy screenplay contest. One of her short stories was short-listed for the inaugural Apollo Writers Festival short story contest.

Besides being a student and travelling, she has had many 'day' jobs to support her writing, filmmaking and acting career. She feels privileged to be a part of the Monash Writers Group.

Austen Lehmann

Austen is a believer in the healing power of stories. A recent university graduate majoring in Literature (that only took him 10 years to complete!), Austen has learnt about and, more importantly, felt the transformative power of stories.

The proud father of three rad children, and husband to a beautiful and strong wife, Austen is constantly surprised by the wonderful life he has. He works hard to be worthy of the gifts the universe has presented him.

Austen hopes his stories help to transform, even if only a little, the lives of others for the better.

Bala Mudaly

Bala Mudaly was born in South Africa and migrated with his wife to Australia thirty years ago. He retired as a psychologist from Monash Health in Dec 2018 at the age of 80. His debut collection of poems and short stories set in Australia, Colours of Hope and Despair, was published in 2018. He's also had a short story, Self-Inflected Pain of the Writer's Kind, published in the Victorian Writer.

Dedicated to learning and mastering the art of creative writing, Bala is now trying his hand at creative non-fiction. He's now in the final stages of completing his memoir, provisionally titled Colour-coated Identities: Growing up Indian South African.

Robert New

Robert has spent too much of his life studying and has earned seven tertiary qualifications. Robert has degrees in psychology, sociology, biology and education, all of which inspire his writing, which has been described as 'educational of the human condition', and 'smart and imaginative'.

Robert's books include *Incite Insight*, *MoveMind* and *Colours of Death: Sergeant Thomas' Casebook*. Robert has chaired the Monash Writers Group since 2017.

Robert is mildly kosmemophobic—meaning he has a fear of jewellery. He has no idea why.

When he was in high school, a dare escalated a little too quickly and Robert made the state final in an interpretive dance competition.

Andy Russell

Over most of his working life Andy Russell was involved with research into intelligent robotics. Some of his robots communicated using puffs of air, licked the floor to follow chemical trails or burrowed through the ground searching for chemical leaks. It was not uncommon for reviewers of his research to complain it was too speculative, perhaps too much like science fiction? Now, in retirement, he has the freedom to explore robotics and science fiction more broadly without any requirement to demonstrate practical implementations.

His debut novel *Intelligent Consent* will be released in early 2020.

Gordon J R Smith

Gordon J R Smith was born in 1927 in Victoria. He qualified as a tradesman fitter and turner in 1949 with the Victorian Railways. He was a Rover Scout and member of the Youth Hostels Association. In 1952 he sailed abroad to the UK on a working and backpacking holiday, returning to Australia in 1953. He worked, married and raised a family on the Kiewa Hydro-Electric Scheme for 10 years. Returning to Melbourne, he worked for 18 years with General Electric. When GE closed, he taught Fluid Power at the Royal Melbourne Institute of Technology, from where he retired in 1993. He has written and published books about his travels abroad and working life.

Erica Tippett

Erica's love of story was developed as a child and she has fond memories of her dad reading bedtime stories every night. An aspiring writer, she was reminded by the passing of her dad that life is too short to just talk about the things you want to do; and has now written a book that she hopes to publish soon. Erica has always had a keen interest in all things international and hopes to promote diversity of voice and perspectives through an upcoming writing project. She loves descriptive writing that gives the reader a true sense of place, and transports them somewhere new.

Karen Wescombe

Once Karen finally put all the thoughts revolving in her head on paper, she has never once given up. That it took her decades to make that decision not being lost on her fans.

From being involved in the PinUp scene to Collectables (and issues with clutter) to Database Marketing to Excellence Training (while throwing in matters of the heart), Karen tries to understand and report on human conditions with empathy and understanding.

A former stand-up comedian who threw it all away when people started laughing at her, she has worked to be the best 'Karen' she can be and she won't quit until she gets it right (no matter how many decades it takes). She hopes you'll support her along this possibly long journey.

This collection of short stories was
written by the members of the Monash
Writers Group, based around the theme
of 'the view from the hill'.

Each writer has interpreted the theme in a unique way
and the collection includes stories from a variety of
genres.

ISBN: 9780994439956

Available to order from bookshops and online retailers
including Amazon.com.
http://a.co/hIx6TBS

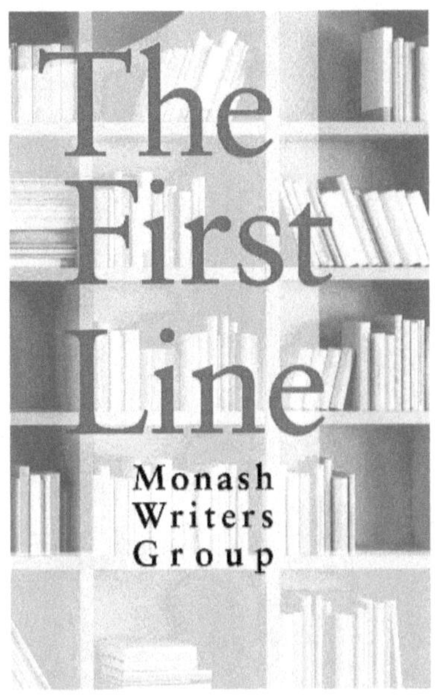

This is a short story anthology by the Monash Writers Group. Each writer has taken the first line of a story they like and used it as the starting point for a new tale. Some lines are famous, others obscure, but the works they have inspired are original and entertaining.

From historical fiction, drama, science fiction, mystery, adventure and literary there is a story in this collection for every reader.

ISBN 9780648327332

Available to order from bookshops and online retailers including Amazon.com.

https://amzn.to/2oNicDj